T0106161

# Punky Rose Bagley

Barbara O'Donnell

iUniverse, Inc.
New York   Bloomington

# Punky Rose Bagley

*iUniverse books may be ordered through booksellers or by contacting:*

*iUniverse*
*1663 Liberty Drive*
*Bloomington, IN 47403*
*www.iuniverse.com*
*1-800-Authors (1-800-288-4677)*

*Because of the dynamic nature of the Internet, any Web addresses or links contained in this book may have changed since publication and may no longer be valid. The views expressed in this work are solely those of the author and do not necessarily reflect the views of the publisher, and the publisher hereby disclaims any responsibility for them.*

*ISBN: 978-1-4502-5767-1 (sc)*
*ISBN: 978-1-4502-5768-8 (ebook)*

*Printed in the United States of America*

*iUniverse rev. date: 9/30/2010*

Ravenswood, Iowa 1975

# Dedication

To the muse who awakened me during the night and introduced me to the remarkable Punky Rose Bagley.

## Thank You

To Jan Stefanki who encouraged me to write the story.

To Annette White Parks, Michael Wilt, and Kermit Cain who read the drafts and helped to shape the story.

And to Alan and Janine Harrington who typed, advised, and were the techs who could launch the book through iuniverse.
Ravenswood, Iowa 1975

# Chapter 1

Punky Rose Bagley hated singing in the children's Sunday School choir. She hated Mr. Dwight Dean Denby waving his pink fists up and down in time to the music. She hated his sidewinder, hissing voice urging the children to "sing, sing, sing!" And she hated the stupid songs such as, "Jesus Loves the Little Children" that the choir was made to sing in harmony over and over again. She stood tall in the back row of the choir, blonde pigtails hanging down her back, wearing a T-shirt with Mickey Mouse on the front, and worn-out jeans. Her tennis shoes had the toes out of them above the rubber soles, and the shoestrings were knotted and dirty. Punky Rose was not at all the image of a good, Christian child singing her heart out for the Lord. She resembled more closely a "tween" who glared back at Mr. Denby and only lip-synced the words of the stupid song. The only reason that Punky Rose Bagley was standing on the choir riser at the Methodist Church pretending to sing songs with the children's choir was because her Great Aunt Haz, short for Hazel, insisted on it, and she had to do what Aunt Haz said, for Aunt Haz was raising her now.

Penelope Rose Bagley had been born in Ravenswood, Iowa, in 1963. Someone had said, "Look at little punky" when she was a few weeks old, and the name had stuck. Her daddy had left when she was six months old, and her momma had gone through one boyfriend after another, until all worn out at thirty, her mind had tipped sideways and couldn't get level again. Now, she lived in a hospital one hundred miles away and could only have visitors once a month. Punky went to live with her Great Aunt Haz, who hadn't welcomed the idea of raising a child. But since there was no one else in the family, Aunt Haz was doing her duty.

In Punky Rose's estimation, she didn't need looking after since she had practically raised herself, her momma being preoccupied. By the time she was four, she could make herself a sandwich and pour herself a glass of milk. By the time she was six, she could set the alarm clock, get herself dressed, and walk down the lane to the school bus stop even in the frigid Iowa winters with ten inches of snow on the ground. At school, she whizzed through kindergarten, first grade, and second grade, all the while her teachers talking about how competent but neglected she was. Her clothes were ill fitting and dirty. She wore tennis shoes even in the winter, and her long, untidy blonde hair was always in her face. Actually, it was her third grade teacher, Miss Bell, who taught her to brush it out straight, part it in the middle with a comb, and braid a pigtail on each side of her head. Punky Rose didn't care about her hair, but she liked Miss Bell, so she learned the grooming technique just to please her.

By the time Punky Rose was in fifth grade with the grizzled Mrs. Henderson, she was getting better at bathing and using the washer-dryer. Still, she seemed like an abandoned child, and all of Mrs. Henderson's attempts to have her mother come to school for a conference didn't work. Nobody at Ravenswood Elementary was surprised to be visited by the county social worker after Punky Rose's mother was carted off to the mental hospital. Punky Rose was going to be cared for by Hazel Limestone, her great aunt, a fine middle aged woman with a decent job, and a trim little home in the south part of town. Everyone felt Punky Rose was going to be much better off. Everyone, that was, except Punky Rose Bagley.

Hazel Limestone was the only surviving sibling in her family. She had been a real "kid" sister, being born to her mother late in life. Most of the family had drifted away to live and pro-create in other states, and as happens in families, bonds began to break down. Once Haz's siblings had gone to God, their children had no interest in Ravenswood, Iowa. But one sister had remained in Ravenswood and raised a daughter, Selma. And according to Haz, she hadn't done a very good job of it. She doted on the girl, spoiled her rotten, and when the girl's father died when she was thirteen, things got worse. Selma had no discipline, and she was boy crazy. Everybody in town talked about her. Haz hated to hear it for love of her sister, not for love of her niece, Selma.

When Haz's sister died of cancer when Selma was nineteen, Selma really went wild. She'd inherited a little money, and a trust fund doled out enough each month to pay rent and buy the basics. Selma never considered going to work, especially after what happened at the ladies boutique when she was a teenager. But that was another story. Haz wanted nothing to do with Selma, and Selma certainly didn't want Haz sniffing around her life. It was only after Selma married a drifter named Bagley and had a daughter, that Haz called her occasionally to ask how the little girl was doing.

The county social worker, Mrs. Gens, had contacted Haz a number of times about the neglected elementary school girl, and each time Haz had agreed to contact Selma and see if there could be an intervention, but nothing came of it. Sometimes Haz drove out to the rented farm house where Selma lived and brought a couple sacks f groceries or some clothes from the Salvation Army shop that she thought might fit Punky Rose. For her part, Punky Rose didn't trust a living soul, and she left the house the few times that Haz had visited. She didn't see any reason to talk to the woman, and her mother certainly hadn't instilled any manners in her, such as thanking her aunt for food or clothing.

One day in the late spring of 1975, Aunt Haz had gotten a call from the county social worker again. "I think that you had better visit your niece," she had said. "The school has sent me out where she lives this week, but she won't come to the door, and Punky Rose makes excuses for her. I think something bad is going on. Would you be able to drive out there this afternoon with me?"

Haz shuddered. Why had this responsibility fallen on her? Hazel Limestone was a small, tidy lady with a heart-shaped face, a sweet smile, and very kind dark eyes. She was a maiden lady, as they say in Iowa, and she lived alone in a small yellow house in the south part of town. Folks said she had the prettiest flower beds in borders around her foundation in the whole south end. She worked for the John Deere Company out on the highway, and everyone said that if the manager dropped dead, Haz Limestone could run the business just fine. She was a dyed-in-the-wool Methodist, a member of the Ladies Aid Society, and she did her duty for charity with precision and pride. She was well-liked, respected, and led an exemplary life, a contented life, with a schedule, and friends, with enough resources to be comfortable. She hated the thought that people even knew that she was Selma Bagley's relation. And now she was being called on to become involved with her niece, to do something more than bring her a few groceries or an old coat for her child. She didn't like it. She didn't like the sound in the social worker's voice.

And so on this May afternoon, Hazel Limestone and Mrs. Gens drove to the farm house and knocked on the door. Punky Rose opened it a crack and peered out at them. "We need to talk to your mother," Aunt Haz said.

"She's sick," Punky Rose said, "she's in bed with the flu or something."

Haz took the door knob in her hand and opened it forcefully. "Now see here, Punky Rose, we need to see your mother. Are you hiding anything? Has something happened?" Punky Rose didn't say a word, but went to sit in a ratty chair in the middle of the room. Haz and Mrs. Gens went to the bedroom off the main room, and there was a catatonic Selma lying in bed staring at the ceiling. She didn't respond to her name. The room smelled awful of urine.

"Oh, my God, what's happened to her," Haz said looking at Mrs. Gens. Mrs. Gens assessed the situation and went right to the phone where she called Dr. Travers and the sheriff's department. Then she looked at the dirty kitchen, the bare refrigerator, the unstocked kitchen shelves. She was shaking her head when she returned to the bedroom and found Haz sitting on one side of the bed, holding Selma's rigid hand, and trying to get her to say something.

"This is bad," Mrs. Gens said. "An ambulance is on its way. She needs to be hospitalized, I'm sure. Dr. Travers and the sheriff will assess the situation, but I think we're looking at commitment, at least for evaluation. Now, what about the girl?"

Haz looked from Selma to the social worker.

"I mean, is there anybody in the family to take her for awhile? Or should I begin to call our emergency foster families?"

Haz looked back at Selma again. "I'll take her," she said softly. "I'll take her for awhile. There is no other family."

The sound of the ambulance could be heard coming down the blacktop highway when Haz stepped out of the bedroom. "Pack your things, Punky Rose," she said, "you'll be staying with me for awhile until your momma gets well."

Punky Rose showed no emotion whatsoever, but she got up and went into a back bedroom where she emerged with a paper grocery sack in one hand. A winter coat was wadded up under her arm. "Is that all you're taking with you?" Aunt Haz asked.

"It's all I got," the girl answered in a stony voice. The ambulance arrived and Mrs. Gens filled the paramedics in on what was to happen to Selma next. Then she motioned to Haz and Punky Rose to go to her car. "I'll drop you off at your place," she told Haz, "then I'll meet with Dr. Travers and begin filling in the paperwork. I'm sure he'll be calling you later. I'm sorry Punky Rose, about this," she added, squinting her eyes into the rearview mirror to assess the girl who had climbed into the back seat. She got no response.

Punky Rose had a sleepless night on Aunt Haz's couch, and Haz woke her early to have a bite of breakfast before she made sure she went off to school. The girl communicated nothing, but she did eat her scrambled eggs and two pieces of toast. "You wearing that to school?" Aunt Haz asked as she eyed the dirty jeans, the ragged T-shirt, and worn out tennies.

"Yeah," the girl said defiantly and then she slumped into silence and never said another word as Haz drove her to the Ravenswood School.

"Walk down to my house when school is out," Haz told her. I get home about 4:00. The back door will be open." Punky Rose exited the car and joined the other kids on the school's sidewalk.

Hazel Limestone had signed the papers to have Selma committed to the Cherokee State Hospital. Then she had called Selma's landlord and told him that Selma was hospitalized and wouldn't be coming back. She had hired some ladies to clean out the house. There wasn't much in the house worth saving except Selma's personal things which she'd asked the cleaning ladies to box up and bring to her house where she stashed the boxes behind the furnace in the basement. She had fixed up the attic room, painting and papering it, putting in a twin bed and a desk and a dresser. She had bought toiletries and some almost-new clothes from the Salvation Army shop for the girl, just jeans and T-shirts, the only thing that Punky Rose would wear. And at the beginning of summer, she'd purchased a good, used bike for her.

Punky Rose had looked at her aunt with questioning eyes, when Haz brought the bike home as if she was trying to understand what her aunt's motivation was. She had silently agreed to her aunt's terms of co-living arrangements. "Now, Punky Rose, we have a schedule around here," her aunt had said. "Up at 7:00, brush your teeth, wash your face, and get to school. When school's out, we'll figure out what you are going to do everyday. At night, I expect you to eat your dinner and take a bath. Once a week, you need to wash that hair, and make sure that you put on clean underwear every day. Put your dirty clothes in the hamper in the bathroom. I'll make a list of chores that I expect you do to every week. On Sundays, we'll go to church, and I think I'll sign you up for the children's choir." Punky Rose made a face, a grimacing face, at that announcement, but she remained silent. She knew she had no options.

Punky Rose had a best friend at school. His name was Sheldon McNamara. They seemed an odd couple. Generally, girls and boys avoided each other until junior high, and then they began walking out as couples. But Sheldon and Punky Rose had found something genuine and wonderful in each other in kindergarten, and the friendship had never come undone. Sheldon was a shy, slim boy with wavy, red hair and glasses. He couldn't see a thing without them. He came from a boisterous clan of McNamaras who lived in a big, frame house two blocks from Aunt Haz. They always seemed to have a party going on as people came and went. The McNamaras had eight children, all high-spirited and full of fun. But in the middle of the clan, there was Sheldon, a quiet, reticent boy who would rather read a book at the public library than play football or tag. His brothers and sisters learned to ignore him, and early on, everybody at Ravenswood Elementary knew that if you bullied Sheldon, Punky Rose would come after you. And everybody was afraid of that, for Punky Rose was the only kindergarten girl to punch out Emmet Clyde on the second week of school. Emmet was a big boy for his age, and loved to lord it over the other kids. But he had been no match for Punky Rose, and her reputation stuck. "Don't mess with Punky Rose," the other kids told each other. "She'll get you good."

It was after choir practice on a hot summer night in 1975, when Punky Rose and Sheldon rode their bikes out to the old gravel pit, which was filled with water. A small river ran through Ravenswood, but if you wanted to really cool off, you went to the gravel pit. The blue, deep water resembled a small lake, and somehow you just felt cooler sitting on the rocks and looking down into the still water and pretending you sat on the shore of somewhere foreign and vast, like the picture post card of Lake Michigan, which Sheldon's Aunt Doe had sent the summer she had visited relatives in Milwaukee.

"Let's ride out to Lake Youcantoo," Punky Rose had called to Sheldon out by the bike rack where he had met her. It was the secret name they had given the gravel pit water taken from a private joke. "I can't do that," Sheldon had often said, and Punky would counter with, "YOU CAN TOO," urging him on to do whatever adventure was currently on her mind. When Punky had learned how to crawl without catching her clothes under the old, barbed wire fence surrounding the gravel pit to keep people out, Sheldon had protested on the outer side of the fence, "I can't get through that."

"You can too," Punky Rose had chided, and after Sheldon struggled through the opening, the kids had both laughed and christened the water Lake YOUCANTOO.

It was about eight p.m., and the sun had almost set. It was muggy and hot and there wasn't a breeze blowing anywhere over the land. The kids crawled under the rusted barbed wire and walked about ten feet to the water's edge. "Let's put our feet in," Punky Rose said, taking off her shoes. The water came from a spring that rippled up through the center of the pit, keeping the water from getting stagnant and keeping it cold. Sheldon was just taking off his shoes and socks when he saw it…a silver bumper of a car just sticking out of the water. Just a silver bumper gently rocking back and forth. "Look at that!" he said in astonishment. Punky looked toward the silvery bumper. Raising her eyes to look at the fence bordering the other side of the lake, she could see where it had been smashed down. Tire tracks went right into the water.

"Holy cats," she said in an amazed voice. Sheldon was looking at it with a sense of horror as the hairs stood up at the base of his neck.

"Let's get out of here," he said in a small voice. "We better get the sheriff." Sheldon fastened up his shoes, and Punky Rose stuffed her feet back into her tennis shoes. She didn't even stop to tie them up, but took off running with Sheldon trailing behind.

Once on the other side of the fence, both kids rode like the devil was behind them, back down the road into town, only one mile but seeming like twenty, and right up to the sheriff's station. Punky Rose was the first one inside. "Is Sheriff Conneally here?" she asked breathlessly, sticking her nose over the counter.

"Why you want to know?" Deputy Henderson asked lazily.

"Because, lard ass, there's a car in the gravel pit," Punky Rose exploded. "A car slammed right through the old fence, and there's tire tracks right into the water." Sheldon coming in behind her backed up her story with a series of headshakes.

"What did you call me, girl?" Deputy Henderson frowned.

"Never mind, there's a car in the gravel pit," Punky Rose almost shouted. "The sheriff needs to know."

"Well, I'll just have to call him at home and tell him all about it," the deputy said, and he began to dial the number. "Sorry to bother you, but there's these two kids here who are reporting something they think they saw at the gravel pit, a car submerged, something like that. They are all excited about it. Yeah, they just came in. O.K. sir, let me know."

"Now you kids go home," Deputy Henderson said to the kids, glaring at Punky Rose, the smart-mouth. "The sheriff is going to drive out there and take a look."

"Yes sir," they said in unison and turned to leave.

"I <u>mean</u> that you go on home. Don't go back out there hanging around," he ordered.

"Got it," Punky Rose said as she swooped back out the door, almost letting it slam in Sheldon's face. "Come on," she yelled at him, picking her bike out of the rack. "Let's get going before it gets too dark."

"Where?" said Sheldon.

"Back out to the gravel pit," Punky Rose spit out.

"But the deputy told us to go home," Sheldon said wistfully, knowing that made little difference to Punky Rose.

"Come on," Punky Rose spat out at him. "To Lake Youcantoo!" And off she sped down the street heading for the gravel road that would take them right back to the pit.

# Chapter 2

The children crouched on their usual side of the fence, after laying their bikes flat in the tall grasses that grew in the field adjacent to the gravel pit. Creeping up on their bellies, they could just make out Sheriff Conneally and a tow truck man talking on the other side of the pit. The silver bumper still shone slightly above the water in the now approaching moonlight. The tow man went to the back of his truck, and took out an inflated raft just big enough for one man. He edged it into the water and got on board. He paddled out to the silver bumper, hauling a big chain and hook with him. He worked to attach the chain to the bumper and began paddling back. The sheriff helped him out of the raft, and the two men stowed the paddles and carried the raft back to the truck.

"What are they going to do?" Sheldon asked excitedly.

"They are going to try and pull the car out of the water," Punky Rose explained. "Now watch."

And sure enough, the tow man started up his truck and very slowly began to creep away from the water. The massive chain came up out of the water as the tension between the car and the truck increased. Ripples appeared all around the bumper as it began moving to the shore as if it could swim by itself. And then, ever so slowly, a vehicle began crawling out of the water, trunk first, mid-section, and front, until it was all the way out of the water and sitting on the graveled incline. The tow man and the sheriff began opening the doors on either side of the car, and water rushed out. And then, the two men hooked it up good and tight and began winching it onto the hydraulic lift. The lift made a faint screeching sound, like the night owl, as the dripping car edged toward the bed of the truck. When the car was in place, the two men talked for a moment, shook hands, and then truck and sheriff's car slowly drove over the wide swath of gravel, through the mashed down barbed wire fence, and headed toward the road on the other side from where Punky Rose and Sheldon watched.

"Maybe there's a body inside," Sheldon said with awe in his voice.

"Naw," said Punky Rose. "If there was a body, they'd a called an ambulance. Might as well go home. The show's over."

"But whose car is it?" Sheldon continued.

"Well, I know that much," Punky Rose said, getting off the ground and heading for her bike. "It's Yip Jenson's maroon sedan. That's for sure."

# Chapter 3

"Punky Rose Bagley!" Aunt Haz yelled as she heard the porch screen door bang shut. "Where have you been? I've been worried to death about you. I don't want you coming home after dark, do you hear me? When it is choir night, I expect you home when the singing is over, not wandering all over town with the Sheldon boy. Yes," she said, seeing the surprised look on Punky Rose's face. "I called the McNamaras, and they said Sheldon wasn't ta home either. I figured that you two was together."

Punky Rose sprawled on the davenport, chewing on the end of one of her braids. "Well, where was the two of you?" her aunt insisted.

"Oh, just riding our bikes," Punky Rose answered, not trying to make anything dramatic out of it.

"Did you hear me about being out after dark?" Aunt Haz asked again, annoyed at the girl.

"Yeah. O.K. Home before dark," Punky Rose said, looking at her aunt mildly.

"All right," Aunt Haz said, getting out of her chair and putting her crocheting down. "Ya want some ice cream before we go ta bed? Got some chocolate tonight."

Punky Rose followed her aunt into the kitchen and sat down at the yellow Formica table. Aunt Haz dished up ice cream and settled across from Punky Rose.

"I saw the sheriff and the tow man bringing Yip Jenson's car into town on the back of the tow truck," Punky Rose said vaguely. "It was all wet and muddy like it'd been in the river or something." She looked down into the chocolate swirls in her dish.

"Yip Jenson's car?" said Aunt Haz. "Are you sure it was his'n?"

"Yep," said Punky Rose. "I knew it cuz he used to come see momma in it."

"Well," said Aunt Haz, looking spiteful. "I guess he did all right, court your momma for a while," she trailed off. "Do ya think they fished it out of the river – whatayoumean it was all wet and muddy?"

"I dunno," said Punky Rose. "It was up on the back of the tow truck and it looked all mucky and water was squishing out of the doors. A little bit of water, not a lot," she added, knowing that she might have said too much.

"You musta got a close look at it," Aunt Haz said, narrowing her eyes at her.

"Well, me and Sheldon just rode our bikes next to the sheriff's yard, and there they was just pulling in. We couldn't help but see."

"Hm," said Aunt Haz. Spoze Mildred Larson will be telling everybody all about it at club tomorrow night. She always knows every little thing that is going on in this town. Now, brush your teeth before you go to bed," she declared. "Don't want no big dentist bills." And with that she took Punky Rose's empty bowl and went to the sink to rinse it out.

Punky Rose brushed her teeth in the downstairs bathroom, went upstairs to put on her pajamas, and lay down on the cool sheets of her little twin bed. Aunt Haz had put fresh linens on the bed just this afternoon, and she always turned them down for Punky Rose. Punky had a little attic room, tucked away above a step stairs. The room had sloping walls and pretty blue wallpaper with white daisies sprinkled all over it. The woodwork around the door and two small windows, one on either end of the room facing each other, was white. An old pine floor shone with wax. Punky Rose had a small twin bed with blue coverlet, a white desk and battered matching chair. Someone had painted them years ago, and some of the paint had rubbed off. There were scratches here and there, but Aunt Haz said they looked "antique." "People were actually taking new furniture and trying to make it look old by scratching it all over," she said. A low-slung dresser sat under one of the windows. Punky's "hanging up things" were downstairs in the hall closet. Because of the slopes, there wasn't a closet in the attic room.

She lay in the dark with the breeze blowing through an open window, feeling drowsy and filled with the goodness of ice cream. "Yip Jenson," she thought. "Old Yip Jenson."

# Chapter 4

Yip Jenson was actually sitting on a deck of his rented cabana house in Dread Water, Florida, that evening, when about ten pm he got a phone call from Sheriff Conneally in Ravenswood. "Yeah, this is Yip. You say what? My car? Fished out of the gravel pit? What on earth, sheriff. What on earth?"

"I don't know how it got there," Sheriff Conneally said back into the receiver. "But I intend to find out. Did anyone have the keys to your garage or the car?"

Yip thought for a moment. "Well, the garage warn't locked," he said. "And I got the keys right here in my pocket. Somebody musta hot-wired it to make it go. Pretty banged up, is it?"

"No," said the sheriff. "I think once it dries out and gets a good cleaning, it might be all right. Haven't looked under the hood yet, to see if there's damage. I'll call you back tomorrow with a report." And with that, he hung up.

"What's that, sweetie?" a young woman with long, mousy-blonde hair parted in the middle, hippy style, said, coming out of the bedroom. Natalie had a drug habit and nowhere else to go, so she had hooked up with Yip the minute he got off the bus and headed down the road toward the cabana that he always rented each year when the snow began to fly in Iowa. He usually came home during the summer, but this year, he had stayed, hating to leave Natalie. It was a good arrangement. He had sex, he had someone to talk to, and as long as he kept her in heroin, she was happy to stay, glad to be off the street, happy to wash his clothes and do the dishes. Yip had made investments and he owned farms, and he didn't mind spending his money now in retirement on this ramshackle cabana house and Natalie's horse. He didn't mind it at all.

But now he had gotten this news. Why would anyone take his car out of his garage back home and drive it into the gravel pit? Some damn fool kid, he supposed, a fool kid with nothing more to do during the summer. Yip hated kids. They always got in the way. When his ex-wife had three, he got rid of her, just bundled her off to a cousin of hers in California, telling her that he'd send a monthly check, but he didn't want her coming back. He made sure that the check was big enough so Laura, his ex-wife, wouldn't squawk, but wouldn't have enough to find a shyster lawyer. Yip had quietly divorced her and sent her a small settlement. For a few years, Laura had sent him pictures of the kids, two girls and a boy, but when Yip didn't respond (even his support checks, small and tidy, were sent by his lawyer), she finally stopped all correspondence. Yip and his lawyer had got her good on charges of prostitution, or so they told her. The dumbfounded Laura, never too quick on the draw, had asked him where he had come up with that idea.

Yip told her that the boys over to Greensboro had laughed about visiting the house when Yip wasn't home, if you had a twenty dollar bill. And by God, he wouldn't be made a laughing stock. He was shipping her and her brats west, and if she raised a fuss, he'd tell the whole town. Laura had an unmarried sister, but no other family. She'd met Yip six years ago at a Grange dance she'd gone to with her sister. She was a lonely, gawky girl with bad teeth, pregnant by somebody else, and only too happy to take up with Yip and do his bidding. Three babies in six years had thickened her waist and slowed her down some, but she still cooked a good meal and kept Yip's house tidy.

This idea of Yip's that she invited other men into the house was crazy. She with the constant washing and cleaning and cooking and watching out for three kids who didn't go to school yet, having men in? It was crazy, yet there was something about the way Yip looked at her when he told her he was sending her away, something that reminded her of her daddy who had beat the shit out of her every chance he got, and all she could do was cower and pack some suitcases and take the children to the bus station.

With Laura and the brats out of the picture, Yip was content to concentrate on making as much money as possible and squiring various ladies around town. All of them were only too happy to be seen on his arm as everyone knew that even though he was divorced, Yip was a good catch. He made lots of money.

"Damn kids," Yip said to Natalie as she lingered in the doorway, swaying slightly and looking at him with big, vacant eyes. "Damn kids vandalized my car back in Ravenswood," he said with contempt. "That was the sheriff calling me to tell me all about it. Damn kids," he said mostly to himself.

"That's nice, sweetie," Natalie nodded. "That's real nice."

Ravenswood, Iowa was a typical, small, Iowa farm town. Its margins were the Raven River on one side, a rising hill on the other, a state black top highway to the north, and corn fields to the south. It was a sweet wooded town established right after the Civil War. Ravenswood had one main street of shops. One side was Kindall's Five and Dime, Taylor's Grocery, Lillians, a ladies dress shop, Hampton's Mens Shop, Feldman's Department Store, the First Iowa Bank and Trust, and the Sheriff's office and jail.

On the other side of the street was the Eateria Restaurant, the Rexall Drug Store, the Ravenswood

Movie Theater, Hap's Jewelry, and the Ravenswood Gazette office. Next, there was the Ravenswood Dairy, the Smoke Shop pool hall and beer joint, and a derelict Victorian monster that once had been a classy hotel. Now, it just sat there, leaning to one side, about ready to fall down. It had been abandoned for years, but for some reason the town never got around to tearing it down.

North of Main Street, one block up was the Ravenswood School which took up a whole block. It housed kindergarten through the high school. Across from the school stood the Methodist Church and next door, the Catholic Church, proud turn of the century edifices through whose doors the whole community went each Sunday, except, of course, for a few reprobates who weren't church goers. Two blocks up from Main Street was the Carnagie Library, two doctors offices, a dentist's office, and a chiropractor, whose office was in his living room. Ten blocks of old mansions and modern big houses of Ravenswood's hoy paloy stretched out to the highway.

Out on the highway, there was the industrial section of town, farm implement dealerships, a Ford and a Chevy dealership, and a few factories that made such things as church pews and modular homes. There was the Dairy Queen, Froggy's Burgers, and Angies Steak House along with two gas stations.

On the south side of town, there were the average houses of the middle class and working class people. As the streets approached Baldwin's corn fields, the houses got smaller and smaller.

The people of Ravenswood were white, church going people, about evenly divided between Democrat and Republican. They were the kind of Americans that kept up their property, helped each other out, were happy to have a washer and dryer by 1975 in their basements, and hoped to buy a new car every five years.

Children's lives in Ravenswood, for the most part, were sheltered and predictable. The center of their lives was the family, and many still kept up the Sunday tradition of meeting at Grandma's house after church for a big feast of baked ham, mashed potatoes, and jello salad. Kids went to school and got a good solid education. At age 18, most graduated and went to work, joined the military, and some even went off to college in Ames or Iowa City.

Kids played football, basketball, and baseball for their school's teams. They sang in the school choir or played in the school band. School and church were the great institutions of the town.

Kids were expected to work part time jobs and did. They were rarely supervised as their lives were extremely safe. Farm kids rode the school bus to town or came in on Saturday nights with their parents. Town kids walked or rode bikes. Few people locked their doors. When boys were sixteen, their families bought them used cars if they were able. Girls depended on boys for rides to events or dates.

Every once in awhile, some kid suffocated in a silo or got killed in a car wreck, racing out on the county gravel roads. The town had its citizens who stayed too long and too late in the Smoke Shop. There were girls who left the high school in the middle of their senior years to go visit their aunts over to Des Moines. Everybody knew what that meant. Some couples barely got married in June before a little Debbie or Jeffry came into the family. There was a county "home" out on county road Old Number Ten, which housed odd people, mentally ill people, or vagrants with no family to take care of them. These people were sequestered and rarely seen in town.

And of course, there was the infamous Yip Jenson, wealthy, divorced, a lady's man and secret distributor of porn in the days when the high school boys thought it really "racy" to look at the women's underwear sections in the Sears catalog. And there were a few floosies like Selma Bagley that the single men in town looked on as fair game.

The cold snowy winters came and went, the soughing soft winds of wet springs, the high humidity, hot summers, and the beautiful mild falls when the trees' leaves turned bright red and gold, and the townspeople raked their yards and burned their leaves in the gutter. That was the season of school starting again, the harvest almost brought in, the canning and preserving done for another year. People got out their storm windows and replaced summer screens. Everybody smelled a little of moth balls as the wools and sweaters were brought out of closets when the turn of the temperature demanded that the citizens keep warm. The cycles of life went on quite unhurried and unchanged and always predictable.

But nothing in Punky Rose Bagley's life had been pleasant or predictable, and it was going to get worse.

# Chapter 5

"Punky Rose! Punky Rose Bagley, git out o that bed, and let's git this day begun," Aunt Haz called up the stairs. Punky Rose turned over and looked at the clock. Eight am. Eight am, and it was a Saturday, too.

"Damn," she thought as she swung her legs over the side of the bed. If she feigned sleep, her aunt would only continue to pester her. Sitting upright, she looked through sleepy eyes out of the window. Bright light flooded the room. "Saturday," she thought. Washing day. Aunt Haz probably had been up for hours sorting dirty clothes into neat piles on the back service porch where the Maytag and dryer reigned. Towels went into the dryer, but Aunt Haz always hung the sheets out on the back line. That was Punky's job, hanging the sheets, folding the underwear and matching the socks coming out of the dryer. By noon, on Saturdays, the laundry was done for another week. And that's when Aunt Haz went to the grocery store for her weekly shopping. Punky Rose usually went with her to read comic books from the racks at the front of the store while Aunt Haz pursed her lips and made big decisions about cuts of meat and fresh vegetables. They carried the groceries home together, and Punky Rose helped Aunt Haz put things away. Then the afternoon was hers to do as she pleased. Perhaps she and Sheldon could go to the pool this afternoon. The day seemed to be getting hot already.

"Want some eggs?" Aunt Haz asked as Punky Rose sauntered into the kitchen, jeans and T-shirt on, and barefooted. "Got some nice fresh ones from Mrs. Barker over ta Greensboro at the farmer's market last night." Aunt Haz didn't wait for an answer but cracked two big brown eggs into a bowl and whisked them around, adding salt and pepper.

"Seems like I'm gittin 'em whether I want them or not," Punky Rose said, cutting her eyes at Aunt Haz.

"Them eggs s good for ya," Aunt Haz said. "Good, brown eggs," and she poured the golden eggs into the big black frying pan. The eggs sizzled, and she stirred them around. "Put some toast in the toaster," she said. "Toast and eggs. You can't beat it for a meal." She bustled about setting the eggs onto a dish and placing it before the girl. A lob of butter sat on a small dish on the table, and Punky Rose cut into it when her aunt handed her the toast. She buttered the browned bread, and slowly ate her breakfast.

The old Maytag on the back porch chugged a contented song.

Breakfast finished and the dishes done, Punky Rose took her place in the back yard hanging sheets. She was almost finished when Sheldon stuck his head around the corner of the house. "Hey," he said.

"Hey," Punky Rose said back.

"Wanna go swimming this afternoon?" she said absent-mindedly, pinning more sheets to the line.

"Sure, why not," Sheldon said. "Meet ya at the pool at one?"

"One will work for me," Punky Rose said over her shoulder to the boy.

O.K., see ya," Sheldon said, and headed back around the house to walk back home.

Punky Rose and Aunt Haz walked uptown to the grocery store. It was an old-fashioned market, small, and easy in which to shop. Aunt Haz whooshed a cart around the store putting things into the cart and consulting her list made the night before. Carefully, she considered canned goods on sale and bought the bargain brands. But when she got to the check out, the trouble began. A snotty high school girl began checking her groceries while Aunt Haz watched like a detective. "Now, Mavis Jo, I don't think that you got the price on that soup right," she said, stopping the girl's rhythm. "The sign below the soup said that it was on sale for $0.63 a can, and you toted up $0.85.

Mavis Jo looked very annoyed. "No, Ma'am, it's $0.85," she said and went for the keys on the cash register again.

"Now, hold on," Aunt Haz interrupted again. "I know that there soup is on sale."

"Was yesterday, but not today," Mavis Jo said flatly. "Maybe they forgot to take the sign down." Aunt Haz held her tongue, but she was as mad as a wet hen, and Punky Rose had to hear about it all the way home.

Aunt Haz settled two bags of groceries in Punky Rose's arms, and taking up two more, the two figures began walking the six blocks home.

"Don't see why they never get the sale price right underneath what's on sale," Aunt Haz muttered as they walked. "I'm sure that soup was on sale. Those smart alec young clerks they hire these days. Why, Alma Watson would always take your word for it if something was on sale. Clerked at the Taylor's Grocery for twenty-five years and never argued with me once over the price of anything. Nowadays, you have to be sharp, I'm telling you, sharp, cuz those little snotty girl clerks will charge you double on everything if they think they can get by with it."

Aunt Haz was clearly out of sorts over the soup incident, and Punky Rose knew that she'd talk about it all afternoon. She was glad to get away from the house after a tuna sandwich lunch, and head straight for the swimming pool.

# Chapter 6

When Sheldon got to the swimming pool at one o'clock it was already filled with screaming kids. Punky Rose was there, too, sitting on the side of the pool, dangling her legs in the deep end. "You got here before me," Sheldon said, as if it wasn't perfectly obvious. Sheldon always made obvious statements that caused Punky Rose to roll her eyes. Sheldon stashed his towel, took off his T-shirt, and adjusted the goggles that he had to wear in the water to be able to see anything. These dangled on a short cord around his neck, and now he pulled them up to his face. But just as they were about to slip into the water, the lifeguard, Hitch Thompson, blew his whistle. Hitch Thompson, all golden boy tan, sat at the top of his stand, letting the high school girls admire him. Every hour on the hour he was supposed to blow his whistle and make all of the kids get out of the pool so he could check for bodies on the bottom (or so Punky

Rose speculated to Sheldon) and skim the floating turds that the little kids were notorious for making, off the top. Hitch would descend his stand, walk around peering into the water, use the skimmer if necessary, and then do a fancy dive off the high board. He'd swim to the side, shake his long, golden curls away from his neck and ears, and calmly climb out of the water and up to the top of his throne again, much to the delight of the high school girls. He'd blow his whistle several times, and all of the kids would race to the edge of the pool and see who could splash the most jumping in.

Punky Rose and Sheldon sat down on the edge of the pool again. "Get in easy," Punky Rose said. "The water's cold today." And with that, both children slithered down into the aqua-blue water. "Let's swim to the other side," Punky Rose suggested. "One, two, three…" and she pushed off the side, side-stroking toward the other side. Sheldon followed. But just as Punky rose was about half-way across a scream of, "Geronimo!" precluded a heavy body making a big, belly splash right on top of her. She was shoved down into the water by the weight of the body, and when she tried to surface the body held her down. She struggled and kicked and finally popped up out of the water, gasping for air. Then she went down again, but this time Sheldon's skinny arm reached out and grabbed her. He pulled her to the side where the spluttered trying to get her breath.

Sheldon helped her out of the pool where she gagged up chlorine water and coughed. Sheldon, looking like a grotesque water bug with his goggles on, surveyed the swimmers. "It was Dexter Hardin," he told her softly, and he pointed at a big blob of a boy dog paddling in the water and splashing everyone that came near him. Punky Rose narrowed her eyes at Dexter. "It was Dexter all right," Sheldon said. "I saw him coming off the diving board. He tried to land on you. I saw him watching you, and then he did a cannonball right on top of you."

Punky Rose looked toward the lifeguard stand, but Hitch Thompson wasn't paying any attention to her end of the pool. "How hard would it be to pants him," she grinned. Sheldon just smiled back and went to the edge of the pool, where he slipped in. Sheldon was just like a seal in the water, a sleek seal, gliding about with hardly a ripple. He surveyed his prey and went underwater.

"Wha?" Dexter yelped before he sank under the surface. "What?" he gurgled as he resurfaced. He whipped his head this way and that as he furiously paddled in place but it was too late. Sheldon had his prize, and after surfacing for one small breath of air, he went underwater again, opened up Dexter's trunks and let a swimmer head right into them. Sheldon yanked them down hard on the swimmer's head and slipped away just as Reilly Ledbetter came up out of the water wearing Dexter's trunks on his head! Reilly yelled, paddled, and tried to get the wretched thing off his head while everybody in the pool began to laugh and point. Reilly pulled the thing on his head off and flung it to the side, while Hitch Thompson blew his whistle three times. Kids began climbing out of the water, all except Dexter Hardin, that is.

"Get out of the pool," the idiot Hitch yelled at Dexter. Even the dumbest second grader knew why Dexter remained in the water, and by now everybody was laughing his/her ass off. Dexter, the blob, sank deeper and deeper into the drink. Finally, Hitch put two and two together, descended his ladder, and fetched the trunks over to Dexter. But Dexter couldn't hang onto the side and pull the trunks on at the same time. He pawed at the clinging fabric and tried to get his feet into the thing, but it was impossible.

Finally, an exasperated Hitch blew his whistle again and told everyone to go into the locker room. Kids hesitated, but Hitch blew his whistle again and yelled at them. Reluctantly they filed into either the boys or girls side doors. Punky Rose and Sheldon joined them, looking completely innocent.

Dexter had to get out of the pool naked, and he was so embarrassed by the whole thing that he wrapped a towel around his waist and butt and trudged right on home without putting the trunks on at all. After he exited the gate, Hitch blew his whistle again, and kids came jamming out of the locker rooms to get back into the water. "Wanna swim from this side of the pool to the other?" Punky Rose said to Sheldon, smiling at him winsomely.

"Why, sure thing," Sheldon said, adjusting his goggles. "Nice day for a swim." And both of them smiled all the rest of the afternoon.

# Chapter 7

Punky Rose sat on Aunt Haz's front porch, slouching in one of the twin wicker chairs. She chewed on the end of one braid, thinking about what was left of the summer. July was almost gone. August would fly by. And by September 1st, she'd be back in school. This year she and Sheldon would begin junior high, and that was a little scary when she really thought about it. They'd have five different teachers and have to put their things in a locker and walk around with armloads of notebooks and books like the high school kids. And Aunt Haz said that she had to dress differently, and act more like a lady, and study hard.

"What had she done this summer?" she thought. She'd make a list. Well, she had read seventeen books, well, really sixteen because the one about the cat and the Buddha she'd read twice. She'd earned her beginning swimming certificate even if she couldn't do much more than sidestroke across the pool. Sheldon was going on for life-saving badges, but she was through with lessons in the Ravenswood pool. She had mowed the lawn for Aunt Haz about every week. She'd helped work in the garden behind the house, planting vegetables and then weeding. Soon everything would be ripe enough to begin bringing into the house and canning. She supposed that she'd help with that too. She'd seen her mother twice, once at the beginning of the summer and once just last week.

She hated going to Cherokee to visit her mother. Aunt Haz usually had to talk to the doctors, and she would leave Punky Rose in the visitor's room sitting beside her bewildered mother who hardly said a thing. Punky Rose would look at the other patients, she would look out the window, but she did not want to look at her mother. Once in awhile, her mother would begin asking her something in a high-pitched, squeaky voice that sounded as if it hadn't been used for a long time. And she'd just whir the words out, speaking so fact that it was impossible to catch their meaning. And then, she'd sink into silence again.

It was torture sitting in that visiting room and being with her mother. But come to think of it, her mother had always been someone to avoid. Punky Rose remembered shreds of her early childhood. She remembered crying a lot. She remembered pulling on her mother's jeans, trying to tell her something, wanting her to read a story, but her mother was always busy, usually entertaining some boyfriend who didn't want Punky Rose around.

"Go outside," her mother would yell, and Punky Rose with snotty nose and spilling eyes, would go outside and sit on the back porch steps, waiting, waiting, waiting for something that never came. The hospital visiting room was much the same.

The worst boyfriend had been the last one, though. Yip Jenson had been a good catch, her mother informed her. And her momma perked up when he was around. And she began fixing her hair every day and gussying up, as she called it. She wore make-up and bright red lipstick, and when Yip called she always had cold beer in the fridge because Yip liked cold beer. Her mother went out with Yip for three months on Wednesday nights and Saturday nights. And she told Punky Rose that they ate supper in fancy restaurants in Fort Henry and went dancing at the Rosewood Ballroom in Arlington. And sometimes, the places that they went for dining and dancing were so far away that she couldn't come home for several days. Punky Rose was not to tell anyone about it. She didn't because the way she saw it, no one would care. And then, there had been a big blow-up, yelling, and door slamming. Punky Rose knew the signs. It happened over and over again to her momma. And when Yip got into his big, maroon Buick and drove away, her momma began her howling. The howling ceased with a few days, but then the strange silence began, and that was when Aunt Haz had come into the picture and packed her momma off to Cherokee and packed Punky Rose off to her own house.

At first, Punky Rose thought she'd have to stay with Aunt Haz for just a few days, but then they got the diagnosis. It wasn't good. Selma was psychotic. Her treatment might take a long time. That's when Haz decided to fix up the attic room. "Now, Punky Rose," she began once afternoon, "you know what I told you yesterday about your momma and all?" The girl just looked at the woman sidewise. "It looks like you won't be going off to live with her anywhere for some time. I've been talking to Mrs. Gens. I don't want the county to put you in no foster home. So, how would you like to live here until… well, until your momma gets well?"

Punky Rose just shrugged. "Well, I guess that isn't a no," her aunt said smiling at her. "Do you like it here?"

"It's O.K." Punky Rose said in the most non-committed voice she could muster.

"Well, then I'm going to fix up that attic room for you," Haz told her. "It don't have a closet but we can figure something out. Guess you don't need a closet with your wardrobe," and she laughed again.

Punky Rose thought back over the past several months. Life was strange, she thought, one minute she was living in that old farm house with her mother, pretending that she didn't care about her mother's boyfriends, and the next minute Yip Jenson was gone and his maroon sedan was sitting in the sheriff's lock-up yard after being pulled out of the gravel pit, and Punky Rose's mother was eating macaroni and cheese at the Cherokee Mental Hospital. It was a strange series of events.

As Punky Rose stared at the street and thought about the summer, Sheldon rode up on his bike. "Ya wanna go to the park?" he asked.

"What for?" Punky Rose said, straightening up and looking at him.

"Cuz, the high school band is gonna practice in the bandstand for the 20th of July celebration," he said. Ravenswood had been founded on July 20, 1888, and the whole town turned out to listen to the mayor make a speech, to the high school band, and to be served fried chicken and potato salad by the Ladies Auxiliary of the Methodist Church. The Kiwanis Club made ice cream by the barrelful, and everybody sat on their picnic blankets and gorged themselves while talking about how lucky they were to live in this town. Punky Rose never thought that she was lucky.

"Well, I guess," she said, thinking that she had nothing else to do this day with Aunt Haz at work and the library not opening until noon. She wasn't in the mood for the swimming pool, and she had no chores to finish for Aunt Haz. "Let me get my bike."

She walked to the back yard where her bike leaned against the porch and walked it back to where Sheldon waited, and then the two children mounted their bikes and rode six blocks away to the Ravenswood Park. Some people had already gathered. Parents who had driven their kids to the band practice, and some little kids with nothing to do like Sheldon and Punky Rose. The band wasn't in uniform, and they looked like ordinary, bored summer kids rather than the dazzling musicians that played those stirring marches on July 20th with the whole town watching. It was getting hot, and boys in T-shirts and girls in fluffy blouses wiped the sweat off of their upper lips and tweedled away on their instruments, getting them prepped for the practice.

And just as Sheldon and Punky Rose settled onto the ground after laying their bikes on the grass, an interesting figure caught Punky Rose's eye. A boy she had never seen before walked right past them and settled into a child's swing to the side of the bandstand. He looked about fourteen or fifteen, was slight yet muscular, and had the longest hair that Punky Rose had ever seen on a boy. He definitely wasn't from around here. Mr. Whistler, the high school principal, wouldn't let any boy have long hair. Neither was it the fashion of the town. "No hippies gonna live here," was what Mr. Whistler had said to the Parent Association when the subject of boys' hair length had come up at one of their meetings. Who was this new boy? Punky Rose wondered.

"Hey, Sheldon," Punky Rose called out to her friend who sat a few feet away. "Look over there. Who's the new boy? Why don't you go over and talk to him?"

"I can't do that," Sheldon said, raising his head and looking at the boy in the swings.

"Youcantoo," Punky laughed. Sheldon pursed his lips and looked at Punky Rose. He knew that he might as well get this over with, for Punky Rose would bug him until he did.

"All right," he sighed, as he got up and slowly headed toward the swings. "Hey," he said to the new boy as he settled into a swing beside him and stuck out his hand. "Sheldon McNamara. I haven't seen you before. Are you new in this town or something?"

"Yeah," the boy said, looking at Sheldon suspiciously, but shaking his hand. "Why do you care?"

"Oh, I don't care, exactly," said Sheldon. "Just thought I'd come over and say hello. Are you going to come to our school in September?"

"Yeah," the boy said.

"So what grade will you be in?" Sheldon questioned.

"Tenth," said the boy, and he began swinging a little.

"Oh, high school," said Sheldon. "Well, don't let Principal Whistler get a hold of you. He'll cut your hair for sure. He hates long hair on guys."

"Thanks for the advice," the boy said.

"Well, good luck on that one," Sheldon said. "That's my friend over there, Punky Rose Bagley. We're going to be in seventh grade this year."

"Oh, yeah?" the boy said. "Probably won't be seeing you then. Junior high and high school don't mix much I'd guess."

"Not too much," said Sheldon. "Hey, my brother Conor is in the tenth grade this year. Maybe you'll meet him and be friends."

"And maybe not," the boy said as he began to swing harder and harder. Sheldon made his way back to Punky Rose. He sat down beside her and tried to look as if he wasn't reporting.

"Wad he say?" she asked.

"Nothing," said Sheldon. "He's going to be in the tenth grade."

"Boy Howdy," Punky Rose exclaimed. "Old man Whistler is gonna have a fit when he sees his hair."

And then the children looked up as the long-haired, new boy slowed his swing down and left the park walking toward Main Street. The sun beat down on Punky Rose and Sheldon. Even the grass felt like it was about to boil. "Let's go home and make some lemonade," Punky Rose said. "The band sounds stupid, if you ask me."

The band was tweedling listlessly through a song. The sun was blazing down on the river and the park, and the children got onto their bikes and slowly rode back to Punky Rose's house.

# Chapter 8

July was finished and August began. Punky Rose and Sheldon found themselves extremely bored. They were read out, swimmed out, and talked out. It was hot, muggy, and miserable, and the days were a thousand hours long. Neither child would voice their longing for school to start again. That would have gone against all summer vacations' codes that they honored, yet secretly, that is what they thought about as they sat on Aunt Haz's back steps after lunch one day.

"I know," Sheldon said, squinting his eyes in the heat. "Let's walk the Indian Trail down by the river. Maybe we'll find arrowheads or something. Wanna give it a try?"

"Why not," Punky Rose replied without too much enthusiasm. "Ain't got nothing else to do."

"Punky Rose and Sheldon wheeled their bikes out to the street and rode the six blocks to the riverside park. They locked their bikes in the bike rack and strode across the park to the left where the remains of the Indian Trail began. The kids walked slowly, squinting at the ground to either side of the trail, looking for the glitter of a bead or an arrowhead, a treasure from the past. Willow trees formed a canopy over their heads, and the grasses and bushes grew thicker and thicker on either side of the trail.

This trail had wound its way along the river in Ravenswood since the pioneer days. At places it disappeared into the water only to start up again twenty feet ahead. The river changed its course especially when there was high water, or at least that is what Mr. Blankenship, the biology teacher, had said. He had told the sixth grade class that when there was low water you could still see remnants of the old trail, and that's when people found the most interesting things that the people who had trudged the trail one hundred years ago had left behind. Kids had walked the trail for a century looking for loot, and some had found it, too. The Ravenswood Historical Society had boxes of displayed stuff at the old farmhouse museum that the school kids visited every year.

"I suppose that there's nothing left to find on this here trail," Punky Rose said almost absent-mindedly to Sheldon. "It's been picked clean after all this time."

"Well, you never know what a good rain might have uncovered," said Sheldon. "Just keep looking."

The kids were deep into the woods by now. The air was cool but very still. They could hear insects buzzing and singing about them, and from time to time the tall weeds hit their faces as they passed by. And then, just as they rounded a little curve, they saw it. Something terrible lay right in their path ten feet up the trail. "Holy cats," Punky Rose exclaimed.

"Oh momma," Sheldon said in a high, squeaky voice. The children stopped up short and just stared ahead of them, frightened, unable to move. "Is he dead?" Sheldon said in a voice that had begun to wheeze.

"I don't know," Punky Rose said. All of a sudden her muscles ached and her head spun, but she forced herself to walk a few more feet ahead. "Holy cats," she said again slowly and quietly, and then she turned back to the white-faced Sheldon. "Let's get out of here," she said. "Run!"

She hadn't had to say that! Sheldon turned and ran as fast as his spindly legs would take him. Punky Rose followed close behind. They ran blindly, ignoring the weeds zapping them in the face or the occasional mucky puddle that they had sidestepped before. They ran and ran until they came to the end of the trail where the park opened before them and the bike rack was in sight. Sheldon slumped onto the grass near the rack and wheezed and coughed. Punky Rose stood over him trying to get her breath. Neither child said one thing to the other for almost five minutes, and then Punky Rose sat down tiredly beside Sheldon. "I think I'm going to throw up," he said between wheezes.

"Put your head between your knees," she commanded him. Sheldon complied and Punky Rose rubbed his back.

"It was a man, just lying there," he said in a soft voice, "a man with a bullet hole in his head, right in the front of his head."

"I never seen him before," Punky Rose said to the air around her. "I never did see that man before. We better go get the sheriff."

The children unlocked their bikes, but both felt too wobbly in the legs to ride them. They walked their bikes along the road silent as sentries until they reached the sheriff's office. Punky Rose sat down on the steps, and Sheldon sat down beside her and began to snuffle out of sheer fear and relief. "Come on, calm down," Punky Rose said after a minute or two of listening to Sheldon. "Let's get this over with."

The children walked into the sheriff's office glumly. The fat deputy saw them coming and gave them the fish eye. "Whada you two want?" he asked suspiciously. "Seen any more cars in the gravel pit?"

"No, this time it's a man's dead body on the Indian Trail," Punky Rose said, staring right at him.

"That's a good one," he said. "Hey, when does school start and the two of you will have something better to do than come in here telling me stories?"

"It ain't a story," Sheldon said. "I wish it was."

There was something about the white-faced boy that made the deputy uneasy. "Hey, sheriff," he called behind him in another room. "You better come out here a minute." Sheriff Conneally lumbered out of his office and up to the reception desk, taking in the children.

"Ain't you the kids that reported the gravel pit incident?" he said, eyeing them closely.

"Yeah," said Punky.

"Well, what is it this time?" he asked not unkindly.

"It's down the Indian Trail," the girl said. "Me and Sheldon was walking the trail thinking that we might find some arrowheads or something, but what we found was a man. A man lying flat on the trail. A man with a bullet hole in his head."

"And who was this man?" the sheriff asked, thinking that this might be some new kind of summer game to get him out of the office.

"I sure don't know," said Punky Rose. "But he's there all right, about twenty minutes down the trail."

"Well," said the sheriff, "I guess that maybe I should go take a look. I'll need you to come with me, of course." Sheldon looked stricken and began to breathe uneasily.

"Hey, can he wait for us at the bike racks?" Punky Rose said, motioning to Sheldon. "He don't need to see that again."

The sheriff began to have a queasy feeling in his stomach. Perhaps this wasn't a game. "Sure," he said. "He can wait at the bike rack with the deputy here. Come on, Henderson, let's get this over with."

Deputy Henderson stood up, looking grumpy. It was air-conditioned in the office, and the afternoon sun was going to be hot. And even in the afternoon heat, skeeters were going to get him, sure as shooten, if he had to go down near that river and the old Indian Trail. But giving a sigh, he locked the front door, put the emergency sign in the window, and followed the children and sheriff out the back door. Checking to see that he had his two way radio, the sheriff motioned the kids into the backseat of the patrol car, climbed into the passenger seat, and the deputy got into the driver's seat and cranked over the motor.

"Drive slow," the sheriff said, "like nothing has happened."

A few minutes later at the park, Sheldon and the deputy sat down in the grass by the bike rack, while Punky Rose led the sheriff down the old trail. No one was in the park. No one boated on the water. And so no one saw the strange company set out on their errand of discovery. By the time Punky Rose and the sheriff came to the place on the trail where the body lay, both were wet with sweat and the sheriff's starched policeman's shirt was limp and dripping. His face was red with exhaustion and adrenalin, and then he stopped behind Punky Rose and looked ahead to where she pointed.

"Red-headed Jasus," was all the sheriff could say. And then he told Punky Rose to start back alone while he looked closer. She was glad to leave him and the terrible scene behind. She walked slowly, solemnly, chewing on the end of one braid and feeling heavier in her heart than she'd ever felt before.

The sheriff made a quick call to the deputy and then went ahead to survey the scene, the man, and the bullet hole in his forehead. The man wore black gabardine pants and a long-sleeved white shirt. He had very white skin and deep black hair. He seemed neat and clean, as if he was going to church or something. His eyes were closed and the tiny hole was neat and clean. There was no sign of a gun in the area. It didn't look like a suicide. The sheriff knelt and felt the man's pockets. No bulges gave away the presence of a wallet. All that the sheriff found was a small blue comb in the man's pants' pocket. He wore no jewelry, not even a watch. And he looked for all the world very peaceful lying there.

But the sheriff knew that when they moved the body, the back of his head would probably come off, and the idea sickened him. He sat down by the side of the trail a few feet away from the man and looked around hard. The only footprints that he saw were his own and Punky Rose Bagley's to one side of the body. The man wore black dress shoes and black socks. The shoes weren't even muddy. How had he gotten here? Did he walk here or was he carried? And if he was carried, where was the evidence of someone else recently walking this trail?

Sheriff Conneally just sat there and thought, until he heard the paramedics that he had ordered and the deputy with the crime scene bag rarely used in Ravenswood, coming down the trail. "Be real careful boys," he told the men coming into the vicinity. "Don't make a mess of the place, and Ted, let's stake this place off." He felt old and tired all of a sudden. "I'm sorry," he said to the corpse as the paramedics moved the body onto a stretcher. The men had tied the corpse's head up tight with gauze before moving him. He now looked like some kind of spooky, Halloween mummy, but the sheriff was grateful that they hadn't lifted him up first. He didn't want to see any mess, not this afternoon.

"Yes sir," he said again, looking down at the bound head. "I'm downright sorry."

# Chapter 9

Deputy Henderson drove Sheldon and Punky Rose back to their houses. Punky Rose stayed in the back of the squad car while the deputy took Sheldon to the door, and talked to his parents for awhile. Punky Rose could see the concern the McNamaras had on their faces as they thanked the deputy and took Sheldon inside, shutting the door after them. And then it was her turn.

When Punky Rose walked through the living room door with Deputy Henderson, Aunt Haz almost had a heart attack. She had barely gotten home from work, and here the police were bringing home her niece. "Oh, my," she said putting her hand to her heart. "What's this girl done?" she asked.

"Oh, she didn't do nothing," Deputy Henderson said. "This girl found something on the Indian Trail that's pretty bad. The sheriff wanted me to talk to you myself about it. It seems that this girl and her little friend…"

"Sheldon," Punky Rose interrupted, standing beside the deputy and looking pale.

"Yes, this girl and Sheldon McNamara went down the Indian Trail this afternoon, and unfortunately, well, I mean, very unfortunately, they found a man lying in the middle of the trail about twenty minutes into the woods. He had been shot in the head. Doesn't seem to be from around here, and sheriff says there's no I.D. on him. It's been a bad afternoon for these kids. I wanted you to know what happened."

"Oh, my God," said Aunt Haz, blanching from hearing the news. "Thanks for letting me know."

"The kids will probably have to be questioned several more times," Deputy Henderson said. "But for right now, there's nothing more to be done."

"Thanks again," Aunt Haz said, holding the screen door open for the deputy. And then she turned to Punky Rose. "Come here, little girl," she said. "You've had quite a day," and she took Punky Rose into her arms and held her tightly. And Punky Rose, who had never been held like this before by Aunt Haz or anyone else, melted into her aunt's embrace and began to sob. Aunt Haz led her to the davenport, where they sat together, hugging while the awful sobbing coming from deep within Punky Rose went on and on. When, finally, the crying lessened, Aunt Haz reached for the tissue box on a nearby table, and helped Punky Rose wipe her face and nose.

"That was good for you," she said in a small, loving voice. "I think that you cried for your momma and everything else in this life. I'm sorry that you had to see this awful thing," she continued. "Oh, honey, I'm so sorry that you had to find that man."

"He was dead," was all that Punky Rose could get out. "He was dead." And then she began crying all over again as Aunt Haz rocked her back and forth and comforted her.

An hour later, she put Punky Rose to bed, something she'd never done before. She kissed her cheek. "It will be all right," she told her. "If you need me in the middle of the night, you just come down and wake me up, you hear?" she said, turning off the light. But the crying had exhausted Punky Rose, and almost immediately she went into a deep, dreamless sleep, a sleep from which she would awake the next morning thinking that everything that she had seen the day before must have been a nightmare and not real.

But Aunt Haz hardly slept at all. A murder. Right here in Ravenswood. Who was this man, and who had killed him? The killer was out there somewhere. Nobody was safe, not at least right now, and how was she going to help Punky Rose deal with what she had seen?

# Chapter 10

The townspeople of Ravenswood, Iowa, were absolutely frightened to death after reading about finding a murder victim on their Indian Trail. No identification had been made weeks after the find, and Punky Rose and Sheldon were celebrities when school began, since they were credited with being the first people on the scene. But Sheriff Conneally and Aunt Haz and Mr. and Mrs. McNamara had told the kids not to talk about what had happened. If anyone asked about it they were to say that the authorities had asked that they remain silent while the investigation continued. And both kids were glad NOT to have to discuss it with anyone.

Parents, who had never worried about their children roaming the town, walking to school alone or to church, accompanied them everywhere, wary about any sightings of strangers. People who had never locked doors or windows in their lives began bolting up, and some people left night-lights on their front porches all night. Aunt Haz was one of them. She was very worried that whoever the murderer was had also read the paper where Punky Rose and Sheldon were named. Would the murderer want to harm the children? Would the murderer wonder if the children had seen anything that the police hadn't?

It was Wednesday night, church children's choir night, and Aunt Haz insisted on walking Punky Rose up to the Methodist Church. She sat in a back pew while Mr. Denby, all pink and flushed, tried to get the choir to stay on tune as he taught them a version of "God's Little Lambs." As usual, Punky Rose was miffed because she had to stand there pretending to sing. This was the dumbest thing that she'd ever had to do in her life. She didn't like going to church. It was the biggest bore, and she certainly didn't want to be standing on the back choir riser looking out at the congregation and singing dim-witted songs. Maybe it was all right for the little kids, but she no longer was a little kid. In fact, since the terrible discovery, she felt as if in some way she had become an adult, a contemporary of Aunt Haz and Sheriff Conneally.

But Aunt Haz was convinced that the children's choir was just where Punky Rose belonged, and she wasn't about to let her loaf at home when practice night came. Now, she sat working a cross-stitch pattern on a pillow front and listening to the music. The choir seemed listless tonight and not very interested in anything that Mr. Denby had to say. Aunt Haz supposed that it was the heat and the end of summer. Nobody had gotten into their "fall" mood yet.

When practice was over, Punky Rose was the first to rush off the riser and join her aunt. "Let's get out of here," she said as Aunt Haz gathered up her sewing bag. Punky Rose did not want Aunt Haz to stand around and talk with the other parents or to Mr. Denby as she had the week before. All of the adults were nervous, and as they clustered together at the end of the practice, they gained a kind of calm as they spoke in euphemisms about the event of the last few weeks.

"Everybody be careful and get home safely," Mr. Denby had remarked as groups began leaving the church. And then he looked around nervously, as he remained the only soul in the building and was responsible for locking up.

Aunt Haz nodded to several other families, and then she took Punky Rose's arm, and they left the church. They walked briskly toward their home. Aunt Haz had brought along a flashlight, and as soon as the lights of Main Street faded, she switched it on. Its little lone beam of light shone on the concrete sidewalk as they hurried on.

Back at the church, Mr. Denby began sorting the music sheets left behind and placing them in file folders. Then he walked across the sanctuary with the stack of music in his hands and disappeared through a door that led to the church offices. He entered the music office, flicked on the light and placed the file folders on his desk.

He was just about to leave, locking the door behind him when he heard a strange noise. He jerked, and his hand closed over the key ring tightly. He looked out into the sanctuary where no one lingered. And then there it was again. It sounded as if someone was clearing his throat of a giant frog. "Hurumph, hurumph," it sounded. Mr. Denby blanched and began shaking. He stepped back into the shadows of his office door and steadied himself by holding onto the doorframe.

"Hurumph," the sound came again.

Now, Mr. Denby tried to consider what to do? He had to go back out to the sanctuary and turn off the lights. He had to walk to the front door and lock it for the night. And then, he had to make his way back in the dark to the little hallway that led to the exit from the back of the building where his car was parked. He couldn't flee the place leaving the lights on and the door unlocked. But the "Hurumph" came again, making his hair stand on end. Sweat trickled down his face, and he held tight to the doorframe.

And then he saw it. A tall someone or something leaving the side alcove and walking to the back of the church. It wore a long black rain slicker with the hood pulled over its head. It went to the back of the church, "hurumphed" one more time even louder, and left through the double doors. Mr. Denby couldn't move, couldn't breathe. He thought he might wet his pants. What on earth had he seen? And then, with a flash of courage, he raced to the double doors, cranked the deadbolt shut, slammed down the light switches, and rushed toward the small hallway where light from his office dimly illuminated his way toward the exit. He didn't stop to turn off the office light. He just flew down the corridor, through the exit door, looked around fearfully, and then made an Olympian dash for his car in the parking lot, got in, roared the engine, and sped for home.

Unbeknownst to Aunt Haz and Punky Rose, the tall figure in the black raincoat was quite interested in them. He'd been watching them for some time, and when they left their house to walk to the church, he'd followed them. He had crouched in the bushes to the back of the church listening to the choir practice and remembering the nights of his childhood when he had practiced with a church choir. That was a long time ago. When Mr. Denby said practice was over, he had lurked to one side of the back wall and watched the people leave. For some reason, he wanted to step back into that church and look around. He wanted to remember better days and church. And that's when he had silently entered and slid to the side of the alcove. He looked around remembering and thinking about how long ago he'd been in a church. He thought about the turn his life had taken when he had left that small town church for adventures in Miami. When Mr. Denby headed toward a hallway on the other side of the church, the figure had held his black hooded raincoat around himself and slipped out the front door, coughing a bit on the church dust. He'd walk down to Aunt Haz's house one more time although he didn't know why. All he knew was that this was the girl that had found the body on the Indian Trail. This was the girl whose mother he was looking for. He'd found out where the mother was, and now, he watched the girl. There was no way to find out if she knew anything unless he confronted her, and he didn't want to bring that kind of attention to himself. It was a false lead, and he knew it. It was probably time to get out of town.

# Chapter 11

M r. Denby sat in the sheriff's office, his little pink hands wringing each other. He hadn't slept all night. And even cuddling with the plump, dimpled Mrs. Denby hadn't made him feel better. At her urging, he had headed for the sheriff's office as soon as it had opened. "I saw it, just saw it walk out of the alcove and down the side aisle. It went right through the front doors, and it made a 'hurumph' sound. It was in a black rain slicker…"

"Wait a minute," the sheriff said. "What do you mean a 'hurumph' sound?"

"Like someone trying to clear his throat. You know, 'hurumph.'" And Mr. Denby imitated the sound. Like that, only louder," he continued with a frightened look on his face. "The rain slicker had a hood, and it was pulled up. Now why would anyone wear a rain slicker when there hasn't been any rain for weeks?" he continued. "And it was tall, too, real tall. Scared me half to death," he shuddered. "Just scared me half to death."

"Well, now, you say that the children and their parents left the church about eight? And did anyone stay around and talk for awhile?"

"Oh, a few people did," Mr. Denby said. "But not for long. And I knew everyone in that church. The alcove is perfectly visible. If someone in a black rain slicker had been sitting over there, everyone would have seen it. I'm telling you, nothing was there after choir practice. I just sorted my choir sheets, and went toward my office, and I couldn't have been in there more than a minute. And when I headed out to the sanctuary to lock up, that's when I first heard the noise. It must have slipped in while I was in the office. Oh, that noise!"

"The 'hurumph'?" the sheriff asked.

"The 'hurumph' exactly," Mr. Denby said. "And then I saw it as it left the alcove."

"Well, thank you, Melvin, for reporting this odd event to me," the sheriff said. "There sure are weird things going on in this town lately. If you see anything like this again, let me know, won't you."

"Oh, yes," Mr. Denby said. "But I'm thinking of canceling choir practice for a few weeks. I just don't think that I'm up to it."

"Say," said the sheriff, "is that Bagley girl in the choir or that McNamara boy?"

"Punky Rose?" Mr. Denby squinted toward the ceiling. "Yes, she's in the choir all right, but I don't see why. She doesn't sing half the time, and I can tell that she doesn't give a switch for the music."

"But not the McNamara boy?"

"Them McNamaras is Catholic," Mr. Denby said with a slight roll of the eyes. Everybody knew that Mr. Denby wasn't keen on the competition of the St. Mary's choir. The Catholic choir had even won first prize at the semi-state finals two years ago. Mr. Denby had never quite gotten over it, them with their papist songs.

"Oh," said the sheriff. "But Punky Rose Bagley was at the choir practice."

"Yes," said Mr. Denby, eyes getting bigger as he began to get the sheriff's drift. "Her Aunt Haz sat in the back, and they left together. I remember that because they was the first ones out the door."

"Don't know if it matters, but I think that I'll have a visit with Hazel Limestone this afternoon. Thanks again, Melvin," and he stood up, indicating that the interview was over.

After lunch, Sheriff Conneally went to the John Deere dealership and strolled about the grounds for a few moments before going inside to talk to Dick Jenson who managed the place. A few moments later Dick went into the clerk's room and motioned to Hazel to come into his office. Aunt Haz had noticed the sheriff, as had everyone else, and his presence made her nervous. Now, she was being singled out to go to the manager's office. "What on earth?" she thought.

Dick Jenson closed the door behind Aunt Haz and asked her to sit down on one of the brown leather chairs that sat opposite his desk. The sheriff sat in the matching one. "Hazel, good to see you," the sheriff said. "Sorry to bother you. I know our talks in the last several weeks have been…well…disconcerting."

"Yes," Aunt Haz said, looking at him closely. "Disconcerting."

"Well, I have something else to talk to you about," the sheriff said. "I hope that it has nothing to do with Punky Rose, but you never know." He told her the story of the tall figure in the rain slicker 'hurumphing' in the church, and Mr. Denby's fright. "Ring any bells?" he asked. "Did you see such a figure or have any idea who it might have been?"

Aunt Haz frowned as she listened. A tall figure in a black rain slicker. Now, what on earth? She hadn't seen a thing as she and Punky Rose had made their way home quickly the night of the choir practice. "I can't think of a thing," she said, but something began to grip the pit of her stomach, and she began to feel a bit peaked.

"Are you all right?" the sheriff asked, noting the whitening of her face.

"Oh, I just hate more mystery with the man on the trail and all," Aunt Haz said. "I just wish that we would get back to normal."

"Well, if you have any thoughts about this figure, could you give me a call?" she sheriff asked.

"Oh, sure," Aunt Haz said. She looked over at Dick Jenson, who was fiddling with a pen.

"And by the way," the sheriff said, almost forgetting. "What can you tell me about Punky Rose's father? I know the sad story about her mother. But what ever happened to Mr. Bagley?"

"Well, you and the rest of the family would like to know that! Aunt Haz said angrily. "He run off when Punky Rose was six months old, and nobody heard from him again. I think that's half what's the matter with Punky Rose's mother. It was so sudden and all."

"Did he have any family around here?" the sheriff asked. "Any folks?"

"Oh, land, no," Aunt Haz said. He was just kind of a drifter. I never knew where he came from. He showed up on a work crew for old man Halliday, you know, the guy with the big dairy herd? And of course, if a boy was no good, Punky Rose's mother would take up with him. They dated for only a few weeks before they went off to Omaha and got married, and then, before you knew it, Punky Rose was on the way. He got fired from Halliday's I hear. I don't know what else he ever did, but when he took off without leaving so much as a five dollar bill, I wasn't surprised."

"Well, that's a too-bad story," the sheriff said. "Good of you to watch over that girl now. Well, thanks for the chat," and with that Sheriff Conneally placed his hat on his head and left the office.

"You know, Dick, Aunt Haz said. "All of a sudden I'm not feeling so good. I think that I'd better go home and lie down."

"O.K." Dick Jenson said. "Just clock out first."

Aunt Haz went to her desk, took her pocketbook out of one of the drawers, and left the plant slowly to drive home and take a rest.

Aunt Haz lay down on her bed after taking an aspirin. What was it about the sheriff's chat that made her so queasy? A dark figure in a rain slicker lurking around? That was crazy. But it was the thought of Punky Rose's father that really started her stomach churning. She had often wondered where he was, why he had left, did he ever remember that sweet pink baby that he had left behind? And would he ever reappear, demanding to see Punky Rose? To see if her mother had prospered? To see if he could beguile Punky Rose's mother one more time?

Haz had never had much time for her niece. It was embarrassing the way she carried on. If she'd been interested in nice boys, it would be one thing. But she always went for the rag-tag, delinquent type, the boys that would never amount to nothing. And sure enough, that is who she ran away and married at age twenty-one, the drifter working on the Halliday farm.

His job was to help milk cows, getting up at four in the morning. But after being married a few months, and expecting the girl to take care of him since she had a small trust fund, it was easier to lie-a-bed of a morning. After a few weeks of this carrying-on, Mr. Halliday fired him.

The drifter wasn't too happy when Punky Rose's mother told him she was pregnant. He had had girls tell him that before, and hearing the dire sentence, he usually moved on in the middle of the night. But this time, he was stuck in this little house, with this blossoming girl, and with nothing to do. The fact that he stayed with her at all until the baby was born was in his mind a magnificent gesture. The little pink squally thing was cute enough, but the girl began spending too much time with the thing leaving him even more lonely for attention. And so, after an especially emotional two weeks where he and the girl fought almost every day, he went out for a pack of cigarettes and never came back. That's what Aunt Haz knew about him. That and his name. Jackson Bagley. Where did he come from? Did he have any folks anywhere? She didn't know, and it was impossible to get any information out of her niece, specially now that her mind had drifted away.

Aunt Haz's niece had grown bored with the bundle of joy, and restless after her husband left, so she began her old routine of flirting and picking up men and bringing them home for entertainment, until the fights she usually picked became too much hassle and they moved on, going back to their former wives or girl friends. Lord knows, Punky Rose had practically raised herself during all these goings-ons. And Haz wasn't at all surprised, when her niece's mental health just fell apart after a bad breakup with Yip Jenson, and she had to be hospitalized.

Oh, if only Punky Rose had NOT decided to wander down the Indian Trail that day. It was as if every time something evil happened, there was Punky Rose. She wasn't in the middle of it. She certainly had nothing to do with it. But there she was, just the same. Yip Jenson's car being driven into the gravel pit lake, the man on the Indian Trail, and now some creep hiding out near the church while Punky Rose sang in the choir. Haz didn't like it. She just didn't like what was happening at all.

# Chapter 12

Selma Bagley sat in a straight-backed chair in Dr. Emmet Swanson's office. She looked off to one side of the doctor's head and began to sing.

Lemon tree is so pretty

And its blossoms are so sweet

But the fruit of the poor lemon

Is impossible to eat.

"What's that?" Dr. Swanson asked. "What about a lemon tree?"

"It's a song, that's all," Selma said dreamily. She fingered her long, pale hair. "It's only a song."

"Well, how are you feeling today, Selma?" Dr. Swanson asked.

"Oh, I'm just fine," Selma answered, never looking at him.

"I hear that you got a letter from your aunt. Seems like your little girl had a scare or something. Can you tell me about it?" Dr. Swanson said.

"Punky Rose?" Selma said, smiling at the air. "Oh that Punky Rose. She's going to be a beauty someday. Course, she'll never be like me. Cleve, my first boyfriend, you know, Cleveland? Terrible name if you ask me. He played baseball on the high school team, and he said I was the prettiest girl in the school. We was in love. Oh, we was hot together that spring time of our junior year. So hot together. But then he went and married that Debbie Sugar in July. I never even knew he was seeing Debbie Sugar. Then they got married, just like that, and Cleve, well he never went back to high school after that. They had a baby at Christmas. Named him Cleveland, too. Stupid name."

"Now, Selma," Dr. Swanson said patiently putting his pen down on the desk. "Let's talk about your little girl, Punky Rose. Tell me about her."

"She sure did like raspberry jam," Selma laughed. "Yes, I always had jam in the house for that girl. I was a good mother, but Hazel says I neglected her. She's wrong. I always had that jam. After Cleve, there was Tom Stevenson and Jack Turner. Tom didn't have a car so it was hard to be alone. Jack had a Ford. We could go driving in that Ford. My momma didn't like either one of them, especially after what Mr. Hanson told her. Mr.

Hanson said he'd never tell my momma nothing if I did as he said, but then he went and told."

"What did he tell your mother?" Dr. Swanson asked, picking up his pen.

"Mr. Hanson owned the furniture store, and he told me that if I came in after he closed up on Saturday nights, and did something with him, he'd give me pretty things, and he'd never tell my momma that he saw me parked with Jack Turner in that Ford at the gravel pit. So I met him, and he showed me his little rosebud thing. I giggled when I saw it. I couldn't help it. And he got all mad and red in the face. He told me to turn around and bend over and then he jiggled and jiggled between my legs. It didn't take long for him to make that high-pitched sound that said it was all over. I jiggled him regular for several months, and he gave me pretty things, scarves, and a bracelet. Stuff like that."

Dr. Swanson had heard this story before. The details were always the same. Selma began to hum the lemon tree tune again while Dr. Swanson waited for her to continue on with her story. Then Selma did what Selma always did at these meetings. She slithered down in the chair, opening wide her legs, and smiling seductively at the doctor.

"Sit up straight, Selma," Dr. Swanson said. "Sit up now and tell me about your daughter. Sit up now," he said again in a fatherly way.

Selma straightened herself in the chair and looked out the window. She said nothing.

"Tell me about your daughter's father," Dr. Swanson said.

"Jackson Bagley," Selma said quietly. "Jackson Bagley. Handsome as all get out. Nobody had a chance with me after I met Jackson Bagley. No, that was it for me all right. Me and Jackson got married and then Punky Rose came along, and I sure was busy taking care of the two of them. And then I couldn't think right no more. Punky cried and I'd ask Jackson if I could fix him a baloney sandwich. Jackson would yell at me and I'd go in and change Punky Rose's diaper. I got the two of them mixed up terrible. And he got madder and madder. And we'd fight, and he'd punch the wall, and then he just went away and I didn't care about nothing no more."

"Not even about your baby?" Dr. Swanson asked.

"Oh, sure, she had her raspberry jam and white bread. I made sure of that. Then Hank Strauss came around for awhile. And Dick Bolger. 'I can do a trick with my dick,' Bolger used to say, like it was the funniest thing in the world, and then I'd make Punky Rose go sit on the step for a while. She'd cry and cry, but I'd pinch her arm and tell her to go air the stink off herself. The fresh air was good for her."

Selma rubbed her hand against the side of her mouth as if remembering something, and then she lazily continued. "Crimson like cherries," she said and smiled. "That's what

Bill Jolt said – that my lips were crimson like cherries. I don't know why he smashed that red lipstick all over my face like he did." And she began to hum "Lemon Tree" again. "I almost got me Yip Jenson. He's the best catch in town. He'll come back. You wait and see. He'll buy me a Cadillac car and take me places. But Punky Rose can't go with us. Yip says he hates kids. And I know for a fact that Punky Rose hates him."

Dr. Swanson scribbled away in his notebook. And then he looked up at Selma who was crooning the song again. "I think that your daughter looks just like you," he said. She's a right pretty little girl, You say she liked raspberry jam?"

"Oh, yeah," Selma smiled, "she sure did like raspberry jam. No, she don't look anything like her father. He had black hair and big gray eyes and beautiful hands. He said his beautiful hands weren't meant to do hard manual labor. He said his fingers were meant to play the piano if only he'd taken lessons. Of course, there was the one flaw, the missing end of his little finger. Got chopped off in some accident or something. He never did like the baby. He called her Punky Skunky, and was always telling me to make her shut up. How was I supposed to do that? And then he was gone."

About this time, a nurse came for Selma. It was time for her to take a pill and have a little nap. Selma stood up wearily and hung her head. "We'll talk again next week," Dr. Swanson said.

Selma listlessly followed the nurse but turned around in the doorway, looked right at Dr. Swanson, and said strongly, "You know he's coming back for me some day, that Jackson Bagley. He's coming back." And then she left, following the nurse down the hall.

Dr. Swanson finished his notes and set his pen aside. In his mind he heard the song Selma had sung, "Lemon tree, oh so pretty," but what was the last line, "Impossible to eat?" Selma and the lemon tree. "Impossible," he thought. It sure was a shame.

# Chapter 13

Gwen McNamara was worried about her boy. Sheldon wasn't sleeping soundly like the rest of her brood. Ever since the Indian Trail incident, he seemed jumpy and fearful. Big dark circles under his eyes became more visible. She called Doctor Wainwright who said that he could prescribe sleeping pills for Sheldon, but Gwen didn't like that idea. Finally, she called Father McGuinness at St. Mary's Rectory and made an appointment.

And so on another sultry day in late August, Sheldon went to the rectory. "How are you doing, Sheldon," Father McGuinness asked. "Sit down there," he motioned to a chair across from his desk. Fr. McGuinness seated himself and folded his hands.

"Oh, I'm fine, Father," Sheldon said.

"Well, your mother tells me that you're having trouble sleeping ever since the Indian Trail situation."

Sheldon lowered his eyes.

"It's O.K., Sheldon," Fr. McGuinness continued. "That would be enough to unsettle anyone. It was a terrible thing. So, how do you feel about it?"

"Kinda scared," Sheldon said in a quiet voice.

"And how is your friend, Punky Rose, doing?" Fr. McGuinness asked.

"You know she's a Methodist," Sheldon said, squinting at the priest.

"Yes, well that's alright. Methodists are fine folks," Fr. McGuinness assured Sheldon.

"Well, Sheriff Conneally said we weren't to say anything to anybody about the Indian Trail," Sheldon said, "but me and Punky, well, we talk about it almost every day. She's scared, too."

"And what are you scared about?" the priest continued.

"I dunno. It's the idea of someone hurting you, shooting you right in the head, and what if whoever did it comes back? And what if they come after Punky Rose and me for finding the body and stuff?"

"Well, Sheldon," the priest said, "I see it this way. Whoever did this terrible thing is hundreds of miles away by now. And he isn't going to come back and hang around the scene of the crime and risk getting caught just to bother some kids who happened to find the body. That doesn't make any sense. I'm sorry that you had to see the side of evil that is in this world right up close like that, but you know, your guardian angel is taking care of you each and every day. When you get to feeling bad, just ask your guardian angel to take extra good care of you, and you'll be all right." And with that Fr. McGuinness sat back in his chair. "So what do you think?" he asked the boy.

Sheldon looked at the priest and nodded his head. He would do just that. "I don't know if Punky Rose believes in guardian angels," he said.

"Well, you could tell her all about yours," the priest said. "She sure seems to be a smart girl who is a good friend."

"Yep," Sheldon said, "we've been best friends since kindergarten. I'll tell her what you said."

"Now, any time that you want to talk some more, you just come over here and ring the bell," Fr. McGuinness said, and Sheldon stood up to go.

"Thank you, Sir," he said, thrusting out his hand to the priest. The man and boy shook hands, and Sheldon left the rectory feeling more relaxed than he had for some time.

The next day Sheldon told Punky Rose all about the guardian angels. "Guardian angels, huh?" said Punky Rose, looking with cat eyes at Sheldon. "Never heard about them before. You really believe in guardian angels?"

"I sure do," said Sheldon. "In my church, they always talk about guardian angels. They're right with you every day of your life, and they help you out and stuff."

"Well, how do you talk to them?" Punky Rose asked.

"Oh, you just talk to them as if they was in the same room with you, even though they're invisible. You just say 'please take care of me today.' Stuff like that. And they always hear your request. That's what Fr. McGuinness said."

"Can't see that it would hurt anything," Punky Rose said, lowering her eyes. "Might as well give it a try."

It was the day before Labor Day, and Punky Rose Bagley sat in the public library writing on a pad of paper. Sheldon slipped in beside her. "Wha cha do'in?" he asked.

"I'm writing a story," she said. "One of them mystery stories, like in True Detective Magazine, only my story has more imagination to it. In my story, these two kids, see, they are riding their bikes down the main street of town, when they see a figure in a black raincoat come out of Laverne's Hair Styling Shop and slink back into the side street. They stop and look in Laverne's window, and they see her lying on the floor in a pool of blood. They run for the sheriff and they tell him about the man in black, but nobody is ever found. All the cash is gone from Laverne's cash drawer and she's as dead as a doorstop. Then, this figure in black turns out to be a spirit, and he kills people all over Iowa and steals their money."

"Wow, what a story," Sheldon said. "Have you got all that written down?"

"Nah," said Punky Rose. "I only got one page, but the rest of the story is in my head. I've decided that I'm going to be a writer and put out dozens of mysteries and get rich and famous and win prizes all over heck."

"I think you could do it," Sheldon said, grinning at her. "I just think that you could do just that. And someday, maybe the best mystery that you can write is the finding on the Indian Trail in Ravenswood, Iowa."

"Wouldn't that be something" Punky Rose mused, smiling at Sheldon. "Finding that body may be the beginning of my writing career."

# Chapter 14

Sheriff Conneally had a secret. At fifty, he decided to write his autobiography. Every day, he'd close the door to his office and speak into a tape recorder. Someday his stories would be told. The tapes were like an oral journal. Someday he'd hire someone to type them all up, and then he'd get an editor from somewhere to take out the junk, and he'd have a grand old book about being a police chief in small town Iowa. On a gloomy August day, he shut his door, and pulled out the tape recorder. He turned it on and began to talk into the mike.

"Ravenswood is a good town," he began. He rubbed his chin, and began again...

"Ravenswood, Iowa, is a good town. I was raised here, of course, but I got away for a while. Went to Chicago and Milwaukee. Learned all bout the big city. But you can have big city life, if you ask me. I got real sick of it quick, and I couldn't wait to sign on as the police chief here in

Ravenswood after Dennis Hopper retired. I had a family by then, a girl from Ravenswood that I took to Chicago and Milwaukee. She was glad to come home, too, and we had two kids by the time we came back.

Now, them kids are all grown up, and just like me, they had to try their hands at the city. One is in Des Moines and the other is in Denver, but I know that they love coming home every summer. We sit up at night, drinking beer and remembering old times and all the people they went to school with. I tell them what I know about what happened to those people. Some turned out just fine, like Alice Hefferstank, who went to the University of Iowa and became a lawyer, or Wilbur Kosser, who became a career Marine. Last time he came home, he had a chest full of medals. But then, there's that poor Bagley woman, can't think of her first name, just wasting away in that mental hospital, her mind just a sieve these days. She sure was a pretty thing, and that may have been her downfall.

And now that Punky Rose of hers seems to be involved in everything that goes wrong around here. We never had a murder that I can remember. Now we find a man dead on the Indian Trail. We never had some guy, unidentified in black, lurking around the church. And now we do. Scared Mr. Denby half to death. And even finding Yip Hanson's car in the quarry. Never had stuff like that when I was growing up. Punky Rose found that one, too.

Most we ever did was tip some farmer's outhouse over on Halloween. That was wild stuff in my day. Now people are locking their doors, and living scared. And I don't like it one bit. I went to the police academy in Waterloo. I take all those update-training courses every fall. I know police work. That I do. And the best thing that a cop can do is nothing…because he's already solved the problems before they start. That's what Dennis Hopper always said, and he was right. But how do you stop a man being murdered on the Indian Trail? A man you can't identify? And if someone is lurking around, some damned fool, how do you stop him in his tracks? Don't even know who to stop. And what if some bored kid decides to sneak around in the middle of the night and steal Yip Jenson's car and drive it into the gravel pit? How can you get to such a kid before he does such a thing? Probably didn't even know Yip. Probably just heard that he wasn't in town at the moment and thought he'd get a big thrill by dumping the car.

I've traced every avenue that the coroner has set up about that murdered man. So far, I can't get any identification from the state or the feds. Nothing remarkable about the poor soul, except that he sure did make someone scared or mad, and somehow he got the end of his little finger, right hand, cut off probably years back when he was a kid. That's what the coroner thinks."

Sheriff Conneally turned off the tape recorder and carefully placed it in his lower desk drawer. Talking things out like this helped clear his mind, helped him consider the problems in a new way. "But damn," he thought. "I just can't seem to make sense of what's been happening in this town these days. Just can't make heads nor tails of any of it."

# Chapter 15

The fall school year began, and seventh grade loomed for Punky Rose Bagley and Sheldon McNamara. Aunt Haz was having a fit because she said Punky Rose needed new school clothes, and Punky Rose disagreed. "What's wrong with my tennis and Mickey Mouse T-shirt?" she asked.

"It's all wore out, that's what's wrong," Aunt Haz said. If you wear that old crap to school, everybody in Ravenswood is going to think that I am refusing to spend money on you."

"Well, save your money," Punky Rose told her, "because I like this old crap. It's mine, and I like it."

And sure enough on the first day of school, Punky Rose wore her worn-out jeans, holes-in-the-toes tennis, and grungy Mickey Mouse t-shirt. The other girls looked spiffy in twill pants, sharp gingham blouses, penny loafers, and white socks. When Mrs. Duncomb called Punky

Rose's name in the seventh grade English class, Marsha Twinning leaned over to her friend, Cheeps Broderick, and whispered, "She should have called her Rag Bagley." Both girls smothered giggles, but by the end of the lunch period, everyone had heard the joke and dares were being made about saying the taunt right to Punky Rose's face.

"Hey, Rag Bagley," Scott Thompson yelled at Punky Rose as school let out. "Got any more of those cool T-shirts?" Everyone got a big laugh out of that. But Punky Rose just turned and squinted at Scott, looking at him like he was from Mars, and then she walked on. Since the name didn't get a rise out of her, it ceased to be funny within a few days. The teasing stopped, but the name stuck.

"Do you think I give a rat's ass if they call me Rag Bagley?" Punky Rose said to Sheldon as they walked home from school one late September day. Sheldon had brought the subject up.

"Well, I just thought you'd want to know," Sheldon said in a sociologist tone of of voice.

"Do you care when the kids call you Squints?" Punky Rose asked.

"No, not really," Sheldon said, pushing the frames of his thick glasses up on his nose.

"Then why do you think I'd care if the kids call me Rag Bagley?" she said.

"Well, I didn't think you'd care as much as just want to know, that's all," he said, trying to play the part of the unbiased reporter.

"Yeah, yeah, yeah," Punky Rose said. "Hey, you want to ride our bikes out to Lake Youcantoo while it is still light?"

"Nah," said Sheldon. "I got too much homework."

"I got all mine done in Mr. Michael's science class," Punky Rose said. "You gotta do something in that dumb class or go crazy. We've been talking about cells for the whole damned week. I don't give a rat's ass about cells."

"You sure say rat's ass a lot," Sheldon observed. "I think that's your favorite saying this year. Rat's ass, rat's ass, rat's ass!" Punky Rose punched him lightly on the shoulder as they came to the cross streets where she would turn right and Sheldon would turn left.

"See ya, Squint," she called back to Sheldon as she turned toward her house.

"See ya Rag Bagley," Sheldon called back.

# Chapter 16

In early October, Mr. Michael told his science class that they would have a special project coming up in a few days. They'd finished cells and bones, and they were going to talk about the reproduction system. Students blushed and squirmed in their seats. But before they got into that, Nurse Northrup wanted to talk to the girls alone, in the auditorium.

Slightly nervous girls lined up to begin their march down the hall to the auditorium where Nurse Northrup awaited them. They shuffled to a row of chairs and sat down. Nurse Northrup stood behind a table on which several bulky items were covered with gym towels. "Now girls," she said as they settled down. "Today we will begin our lecture on how to take care of a baby."

"Why do we have to do that?" Dorothy Sayers asked.

"Because sooner or later, you are all going to be little mothers, and you might as well know the basics right now. Some of you have baby brothers or sisters, and some of you baby sit. You must know about babies. Now, once you have a baby," she began, but Dorothy Sayers interrupted again.

"Are babies born the same way as puppies?" she asked. "My dog had puppies last spring."

"We are not discussing the birthing process," Nurse Northrup said, all red in the face. "That will come later. My job is to tell you how to take care of a baby. Now, write all this down in your science notebooks." Girls began opening their notebooks and finding pencils. "Equipment, girls. Equipment is important. You will need three dozen flannel diapers, you can't get by with less, then baby T-shirts, ten receiving blankets, a dozen bottles, and a big sterilizing kettle like this." And she whisked the towel off a big kettle that looked like the one in which Aunt Haz canned tomatoes. Punky Rose took notes.

"You will need to sterilize the bottles between feedings, not just wash them, but sterilize them. You will buy milk and formula in powdered form, like this," and she held up a can, "and mix it well. Then after feeding the baby, you will rinse, wash, and sterilize…the nipples and the bottle by boiling them in this kettle." At the word nipple, several girls giggled and Nurse Northrup gave them a withering look. "And girls," she continued, "don't do what your grandmother did and breast feed. It will ruin your figures." At the word breast, everyone settled down and looked embarrassed.

"All right, you have your equipment and you've brought your baby home from the hospital. Next, you have to find a place for the baby to sleep. You may have a basket or a cradle lent to you by relatives, but if you don't, a dresser drawer will do. You just slide the drawer out, put an army blanket in the bottom, a receiving blanket on top, making sure that the sides are covered so the baby won't get hurt, and you'll have a perfect baby bed."

Everyone began to look confused. "Any questions?" Nurse Northrop said in a tone of voice that invited none. "Good, now on to feeding the baby. You sit the bottles of milk in hot water until the milk is luke warm. Squeeze a few drops out on your wrist to check for the temperature. Then place the baby in your arm, like this," and at this point she whisked a doll out from under another towel. "Put the nipple of the bottle in the baby's mouth, and the baby will do the rest. And questions?"

Dorothy Sayers raised her hand. "Yes, Dorothy," Nurse Northrup said tiredly.

"Don't you have to burp babies or something? My little brother pukes up all the time."

"Throws up, Dorothy, throws up. Use proper vocabulary," Nurse Northrup said. "Yes, after the baby drinks his or her bottle, just put them over your shoulder like this and pat their backs. It will help them get rid of gas or air bubbles." At the word gas, many girls began to chortle, and Dorothy Sayers made farting sounds with her mouth on her arm. "Stop that laughing!" demanded Nurse Northrup.

It took a few minutes for things to calm down. "Now," said Nurse Northrup, "we will go over how to properly diaper a baby. You must keep your baby absolutely clean at all times. Never let a baby linger in wet or poop diapers." Smothered giggles were heard all over the room. "A baby's bottom must be clean at all times, and then you put Johnson's talcum powder on the bottom," and with that Nurse Northrup shook a cloud of powder all over the doll. Girls broke up.

"Do you clean the poop off with toilet paper?" Dorothy called out.

"Of course not," Nurse Northrop yelled at the ceiling. "You use little wash cloths, little wet wash cloths."

"Was that in our equipment list?" Dorothy asked.

"Yes, well I think so, well, add it if I didn't mention it," Nurse Northrop spit out. "Take the poop diaper off, rinse it in the toilet, wash the baby's bottom and powder it before applying a clean diaper. Then, always soak the diaper and wash the cloth in Clorox before putting them into the washing machine.

"Now, let's go on to the baby's bath. You must give the baby a daily bath, and there's no better place than in the kitchen sink. Fill it with water and bubble bath if you want, test the water with your elbow, like this," and she leaned into a large basin which she uncovered, "and hold the baby's neck like this," and she demonstrated with the powdery doll. "You wash the baby with your other hand. Never let go of a baby in the water, girls, NEVER," she demanded. "Oh, I can't tell you the horrible stories of girls who did not hold their babies properly in the bath water. A child can drown in a matter of seconds. After you've washed the baby, lay it on a clean towel on the drain board, pat it dry and put more powder on it. And that's all there is to it. You will have a clean, well-fed baby if you follow my advice." She stepped back from the table, her demonstration over.

"When are we going to have this here baby?" Mildred Coffee asked nervously. "I mean, is there a certain age or something?"

"Well, girls, you will finish seventh and eighth grades and go on to high school. And then you'll fall in love with a nice boy, and get married, and then you'll have a baby."

"But is it like having those puppies?" Dorothy asked again.

"Dorothy, I do with that you'd stop talking about those damned puppies," Nurse Northrup sputtered. Dorothy and Mildred squinted at each other in confusion.

"Well," Mildred said to the group, "my mother says that you have to have a period and everything before you can have a baby." Now the whole group just broke up, laughing uncontrollably. Nurse Northrop whacked the table with a ruler real hard five times. "Class dismissed," she roared and walked straight for the door.

Punky Rose sat listening to all of this strange information. She couldn't make heads or tails out of this stupid talk about taking care of a baby. She wondered who on earth would be interested in such things. And she wondered if her mother had ruined her breasts feeding her or had she used a bottle. Had she kept her bottom clean? Had she sterilized everything? The whole topic made her restless for the rest of the day.

# Chapter 17

"Spermatozoa," Sheldon McNamara said to Punky Rose as they walked home from school. "My mother said spermatozoa makes a baby. It combines with an egg, and then after nine months, you have a baby. I think that's right."

"But where does it come from?" Punky Rose asked. "Do you buy it at the drug store or something?"

"No, it comes out of a boy's weenie."

"Weenie?" said Punky Rose incredulously. "That thing you pee with? You mean if you pee on a girl, that stuff gets on a girl's egg?" I don't think I have any eggs. I'm not a chicken."

Neither Sheldon or Punky Rose thought it was one bit funny. In fact, both were dismayed about the whole idea. "Well, I think my mother said you had eggs in your stomach, or something like that, and then it can happen."

"So, you're telling me that if we're out at Lake Youcantoo, and you have to take a leak, and the wind is blowing, and I got some pee on my leg or stomach or something, I'd get a baby?"

"Yeah," Sheldon nodded, "it's something like that."

"Ye gods," Punky Rose said slowly. "This could be serious. For god's sake, Sheldon, don't pee in the wind around me."

Aunt Haz was polishing the coffee table in the living room with furniture polish when Punky Rose came in from school and slumped on the couch. "What's eating you?" Aunt Haz asked.

"Well, Nurse Northrup gave us a talking to about babies," she said. "How to keep them clean and make them a bed in a dresser drawer."

"A dresser drawer?" asked Aunt Haz, sitting down in her rocking chair. "Whadayou mean, a dresser drawer?"

"Well, she said that if you are just starting out in life and have a baby and don't have a crib for it, you can make it a bed in a dresser drawer."

"Oh, I see," Aunt Haz said frowning.

"And Dorothy Sayers seems to think that having a baby is like her dog having puppies, but Nurse Northrup didn't want to talk about that. And then, Sheldon said that there's spermatoadspool in a boy's pee and if it gets on a girl, she'll have a baby cuz her egg will get hit."

"What?" Aunt Haz squawked.

"Well, it's his story, not mine," Punky Rose assured her.

Aunt Haz began to chuckle. "Oh, Punky Rose, I guess you will be thirteen soon," she said. "I think that it's time to have a talk about the birds and the bees. Or puppies," and she began wiping her eyes with a corner of her polishing rag. "You meet a boy and fall in love and get married. Then, well, then you sleep in the same bed. And you cuddle, you see. You cuddle. And things happen. And then you have a baby." She could tell that Punky Rose didn't quite get it. "Or to put it another way, boys and girls are different, you know, down here," and she pointed to her lap. Punky Rose began to look at her strangely.

"I know that," Punky Rose said. "Sheldon has a weenie that he pees out of. I've seen him and his brothers having a contest to see how far they would shoot their pee. His brother always wins."

"Why, Punky Rose Bagley," Aunt Haz said, alarmed. "I hope that you haven't spent time with those McNamara boys having a peeing contest!"

"Nah, I just saw them do it once down at the park when no one else was around."

"Well," said Aunt Haz, "I think that the time has come to call Dr. Calvine, and have him go over the facts of life with you. I'm calling him right here and now and making an appointment."

Several days later after school, Punky Rose Bagley stopped at Dr. Calvine's office on Main Street on her way home, and his nurse ushered her into his office. "Well," the white-haired gentleman said, when he saw her. "Your Aunt Haz thinks it about time you learn about reproduction. Is that it?"

"I guess so," Punky Rose said, thoroughly embarrassed. Dr. Calvine saw her strained face.

"Now Punky Rose, this is the most natural thing in the world. Nothing to worry about. Now, I'm just going to pull down this chart on the wall, and then I'll explain everything."

An hour later, a white-faced Punky Rose left the doctor's office deep in her own thoughts. She walked down to the library and sat on the steps. "Rat's ass," she said to herself. "Oh, rat's ass."

# Chapter 18

Late October came to Ravenswood, and the temperature dropped. Aunt Haz got out her winter clothes from the depths of a downstairs closed and with them came Punky Rose's old navy wool coat that had been bought by her mother years before at the Salvation Army store on the edge of town. "Try this one," Aunt Haz told Punky Rose, and Punky Rose tried, but the coat was a tight squeeze, and the arms were quite short, and she couldn't quite get it buttoned. "That thing is a rag and now it's too small," she said. "I know how you feel about new clothes, but that thing has got to go."

The next morning was quite crisp, and Punky Rose pulled an old gray sweatshirt over her Mickey Mouse T-shirt before she went to school. Aunt Haz went to her job, but on her lunch hour, she went shopping at Feldmen's Department Store on Main Street. She went through the racks of children's and teenager's coats, checking out the workmanship and the price tags. Finally, she chose a coat, knit cap, and pair of mittens. "Your daughter will really like this outfit," the saleswoman said, and Aunt Haz pursed her lips.

"You don't know Punky Rose," she said, frowning.

When Punky Rose returned home at four, Aunt Haz was already there. "Wasn't much business today," she announced, "so I took an hour off to come home early. My feet are killing me, anyway. Oh, there's a bag over there on the kitchen table with something in it for you."

Punky Rose walked into the kitchen and picked up the bag as if it might be filled with horseshit or something. She held it away from her body as she came back into the living room. "Well, open it up," Aunt Haz said, trying not to sound too interested.

Punky Rose stuck her hand deep into the bag and pulled out a wool, fuzzy, bright red coat. She stood there looking at it, but said nothing. "That's not all," Aunt Haz said. Punky Rose dipped her hand into the bag again and pulled out a white knit cap which you could pull down over your ears, and a pair of red and white striped mittens. "Well, try on that coat," said Aunt Haz.

Punky Rose unbuttoned the front of the coat and slid into it. It was a perfect fit. Then she tried on the cap and mittens. And there she stood, silent, just looking down at the mittens, not saying a word. "Go into my bedroom and look in the bureau mirror," Aunt Haz suggested. Punky Rose walked slowly across the room, down the hall, and into her Aunt's bedroom. She stood before the mirror just staring at herself. Aunt Haz came in behind her. "My, that looks just fine," she said. "Real pretty. Turn around this way and look at the side view." Punky Rose obliged, but still said nothing.

"Look how nice that red goes with your complexion and blonde hair," Aunt Haz said.

And then, Punky Rose did a strange thing. She sat down on the edge of Aunt Haz's bed and began to cry.

Punky Rose snuffled and tears ran down her cheeks. Aunt Haz grabbed up some tissues from the night stand and handed them to her. Punky Rose took off the mittens and wiped her eyes, but more tears took the place of those that she wiped from her face. "What's the matter?" Aunt Haz said gently as she sat down beside her. "Don't you like the coat?" Punky Rose wagged her head NO, but that wasn't what she meant. So she wagged it up and down. And then the confusion of the moment became so silly that she began to laugh, and Aunt Haz laughed with her. The laugh seemed to come from some deep funny place down inside her, and she just couldn't stop for some time. All the giggling made her cry even more, and she sobbed, and then laughed, sobbed and laughed, until Aunt Haz said, "Oh, stop Punky Rose, I can't get my breath."

Punky Rose blew her nose into a tissue, and Aunt Haz did the same. And then the aunt and niece just sat there for a few moments. Punky Rose stroked one arm of the lovely, soft coat, and then she looked toward her aunt. "It's awful nice," she said. "It sure is."

A few weeks later when the temperature really took a dip, Punky Rose wore her new coat to school. "Look at Rag Bagley," a snotty girl said. "Looks like she's got a new coat." But Punky Rose kept walking down the hall with a big smirk on her face. All that day, she carried the coat with her wherever she went, and by 11:00, nobody made comments about it anymore.

"That sure is a nice coat," Sheldon McNamara said as they trudged home together.

"Oh, rat's ass," Punky Rose said, but on her face was a great, big smile.

# Chapter 19

It was visiting day at Cherokee Hospital, and Punky Rose and Aunt Haz sat on the metal folding chairs in the visitor's room and waited for Punky Rose's momma to appear. It seemed as if they'd waited a long, long time before she came through the door. There were dark shadows under her eyes. Her silky hair was pinned back behind her ear with a bobby pin and she wore the hospital gray, lifeless, cotton dress. She walked slowly toward them and looked around as if afraid of something before sitting down on one of the chairs.

"There you are," Aunt Haz said. "And how are you feeling today?" Aunt Haz took the woman's hand and patted it, but the woman looked down into her lap and didn't reply. "Look who is here?" Aunt Haz continued. "It's your own Punky Rose. Isn't she getting to be a big girl these days?"

The woman raised her head and squinted at Punky Rose as if she didn't quite remember who she was. "Punky Rose?" she questioned. "Your little girl," Aunt Haz said, patting her hand again. "Your own little girl." The woman didn't respond. "Ah, well, why don't the two of you get reacquainted for a minute while I talk to your doctor," Aunt Haz said. "Say something to your momma, Punky Rose," she added, before getting up and walking away toward the door.

"Hi, momma," Punky Rose said in an embarrassed voice. The woman looked at her more closely, bending a little toward the girl. "Momma, I have a question," said Punky Rose. "Just a little question." The woman began to smile slightly.

"I have answers," she said. "Shhh, don't let anyone know. But I have answers," and she nodded her head and bent into Punky Rose's again.

"It's about my daddy," she began. "What was he like? Do I look like him? Where did he go anyhow?" When the woman didn't answer, Punky Rose looked away. "I just wanted to know," she said in a trailing voice. And then the woman and the girl sat in silence for awhile.

A few older children played on the other side of the room. An old lady read to a young man with the mind of a child. Sunlight came through the long, narrow windows, stabbing sunspots on the waxed floor. An old man shuffled past. "I can't shit," he said to no one in particular. "I just can't shit." And Punky Rose had to smile at that and shake her head.

"It's true," her momma said. "Old George there can't shit. It's terrible. It's terrible what they do to us here. They make us stand in the showers for hours. All that water, hot water, too much water. I hate all that water, I'm telling ya, I hate that water," she said now with rising voice. "I hate that water," she began to yell.

"Momma, momma, it's all right," said Punky Rose as a nurse in a white uniform strode toward them.

"Calm down," the nurse said, slightly shaking her mother's shoulders.

Punky Rose saw something flash in her mother's eyes. "You don't want anyone to know," she spat at the nurse. "You don't have any secrets of your own, but you don't want anyone to know mine. Well, I'm going to tell, tell everything," and she jumped out of her chair and went after the nurse, grabbing and pushing and shoving until an orderly, a big, strong man with greased-back hair, rushed at her and gave her a bear hold from behind, lifting her off the floor, and almost waltz-like, danced her across the floor and out into the hallway.

Aunt Haz had come back into the room when she heard all the commotion, and she saw the orderly take her niece through the doors. She walked tiredly over to Punky Rose who sat rigidly on her chair. "Let's get out of here," she said. "Maybe she'll be better another day, and we'll be able to visit for awhile. Come on, Punky Rose," and the two of them walked out of the visiting room together, the eyes of everyone in the room focused on their exit.

# Chapter 20

Jake Barnside liked Aunt Theresa good enough, but he thought that Ravenswood was a dive. After Stockton, California, this town was just plain boring. His aunt had trimmed his hair before school started, but it still was longer than any other boy's at Ravenswood High School. Jake was good at school without putting too much effort into it, and he was an absolute loner, so he didn't join clubs or go out for sports or make friends. His aunt had gotten him a part-time job at the creamery after school, and so his days were filled with going to school, and carrying crates of newly washed bottles to the assembly room where the milk and cream were splashed by the big machines back into the bottles. Once the lids were sealed on tight, Jake carried cartons of them back out to the refrigeration room, where they'd be kept cool until the men who delivered them to the citizen's doors every morning picked them up for the day. All of this was fine with Jake. He liked to be busy.

At night after supper, he read mystery novels by the carload, paperbacks that he bought at the Rexal Drug Store, listened to the news on the radio, and went to bed by 10:00. "He's a good boy," his aunt told her friends. "Never gives me a nickel's worth of trouble."

But Jake had begun to suspect that someone was watching him at school and on Saturday afternoons when he raked his aunt's lawn of the autumn leaves. There was a wisp around the corner, a kid riding by on a bike going a little too fast. Again and again, her would spot her, a girl with long, blonde braids who wore funny, old clothes like the worn-out things that you put on during the hottest days in the summer. He began to wonder who she was, as he saw her when he left the Creamery one Tuesday in the late afternoon. The sun was going down by 6:00 these days, so that by 5:30 when he got off work, it was getting downright dark outside. Jake began walking toward his aunt's house, and the kid who had been watching him in the Creamery parking lot began to ride her bike slowly after him.

Turning a corner, he saw that she was about half a block behind him, and with a wild twist, he headed right for her running as fast as he could. Punky Rose didn't have a chance. She couldn't get her bike turned around fast enough, and while she tried, Jake grabbed at her arm.

"What are you following me for?" he yelled at her as she struggled to get rid of his grip. "What for?"

"I aint' following you," she yelled back. "Can't a girl ride her bike on the street without having some jackass grab at her?"

With that Jake dropped his hand, and the two stared at each other, Jake big and muscled with jet black shaggy hair and squinting gray eyes; Punky Rose with her heart-shaped face, cornflower blue eyes, and sandy blonde braids. Neither said a word for a moment, but they just looked at each other. And then Punky Rose grinned and stuck out her hand. "Punky Rose Bagley," she said.

The boy didn't seem to know what to do now, but finally in confusion, he shook her hand. "Jake Barnside," he said.

"Seen you at the park this summer," Punky Rose said. "I was there with my friend, Sheldon, and he came and swang beside you for awhile."

"That little red headed squint with the glasses," Jake said.

"That's him," Punky Rose said. "And watch who yer calling a squint."

"No offense," Jake said.

"Hey, Sheldon says that you live with your Aunt Theresa over on Lilac Street."

"Yeah," Jake said. "What's it to ya?"

"Nothing," said Punky Rose. "I live with my aunt, too. My momma, well, she's away for awhile. I didn't like it at first, but I guess it's O.K. now."

"Yeah," Jake said, "my aunt's O.K. too. My mom's in California with my sisters, but I just got tired of being there, so she shipped me back to my Aunt Theresa for awhile. It's hard for my mom to make ends meet to take care of three kids," he added as an explanation.

"Sure, I get it," Punky Rose said. "My momma can't make ends meet either."

The two became quiet then, looking at the ground, feeling uncomfortable, but not wanting to leave. "Well, maybe sometime you can come out to Lake Youcantoo with my friend, Sheldon, and me," Punky Rose said.

"Where's that?" Jake asked now, looking straight at Punky Rose.

"Oh, it's the gravel pit, but we call it Lake Youcantoo," Punky Rose said. "It's great in the summer, and it gets frozen in the winter, but my aunt says she'll kill me if I walk out on the ice. Two boys went right through it when she was a girl, and they never could find them until spring. Last summer, Sheldon and me found a car someone had driven into the gravel pit, a big maroon Buick. We found it first, saw its bumper right there sticking out of the water."

"Huh," said Jake now, squinting his eyes at Punky Rose. "Who'd want to drive a car into the gravel pit?"

"I don't know," said Punky Rose, "but somebody wanted to get at old Yip Jenson. That's my guess. And he deserves it, too. He's a nasty, old man."

"Where's this Yip at?" Jake asked. "Didn't he hear someone taking his car right out of the garage?"

"Nah," said Punky Rose. "He's in Dread Water, Florida. Heard the sheriff say that one."

"Well, screw him, then," Jake said and smiled, really smiled at Punky Rose. "Yeah, sure, sometime we'll take a little bike ride out to that gravel pit."

"Well, see ya," Punky Rose said, as she turned her bike around.

"Yeah, see ya," Jake said, turning toward home.

Punky Rose whooshed down the street all giggly and happy inside. She'd been curious about that new boy ever since she'd first seen him in the park during the summer. She'd seen him on the first day of school as everybody walked down the old school walkway, the high schoolers going left and the junior higher going right to their respective buildings. She'd seen that boy going into the Creamery after school and leaving two hours later. And she was just plain curious about that boy. But it felt different than being curious about how the cells in the body split, as her science teacher told her they did. It was different than being curious about how a good book was going to end. There was an edge to this curiosity, a sharp feeling in your stomach-kind-of-curiosity about this boy.

As she came to her house and got off her bike to back it into the garage, her heard about stopped. What had Jake said, "…didn't Yip hear someone taking the car out of his garage?" How did he know that Yip even had a garage or that the car had been inside it? "Rat's ass," she said to herself as she closed Aunt Haz's garage door and walked toward the back door.

# Chapter 21

It was almost October 31, Samhain, Halloween, and everyone at Ravenswood Jr. High was going to a party. Mr. Dwight Denby, choirmaster at the Methodist Church was planning a party for the children's choir members, and Aunt Haz thought that Punky Rose should attend. "Can Sheldon go with me, him being a Catholic and all?" Punky Rose asked.

"Well," said Aunt Haz slowly, "I don't see why not. I'll just call Mr. Denby and ask."

Mr. Denby rolled his eyes at his wife when Aunt Haz asked her question over the phone, but he really couldn't say no without seeming prejudiced against Catholics, which in reality he was. At least it would keep Punky Rose busy, and she wouldn't ruin the party with her attitude. Aunt Haz seemed mightily pleased with his response, and she reported the conversation to Punky Rose.

"Now, Punky," she said, "you'll have to wear a costume. Everyone is required to come in costume. What would you like to wear, anyway?" Punky Rose slouched into a kitchen chair and thought about it.

"Well, how about a pirate?" she said, brightening. "Sheldon and me could go as pirates. We could wear a patch over one eye and everything."

"Hm," said Aunt Haz. "I suppose with an old man's shirt and overalls, we could make a costume. If the pant legs were really big, we could make them look billowy. You could wear my old work rubber boots, and we could push the pants into them, then fluff them out a little bit. Could do the same with a white shirt. We could tie a red handkerchief around your neck, and I could make a black patch for your eye. But a hat. Now, there's a challenge. Where could we find a hat? I wonder if Mr. McNamara has any old fedoras that we could pin up the sides and make some kind of pirate's hat? Think I'll call Sheldon's mother. And I'll tell her that Sheldon is welcome to the party too." And she went o the phone.

The next dayAunt Haz went o the Salvation Army store and found everything she needed for the costumes. Mrs. McNamara had sent over two old hats, one in black felt and the other made of straw. "It's all that I could put my hands on," she said. But Aunt Haz was a whiz with safety pins and a little needle and thread, and the hats turned out with triangular-shaped brims that looked just fine.

The night of the party, Punky Rose and Sheldon dressed up in their costumes. "Hey, walk like yer swashbuckling," Punky Rose said to Sheldon as he stood in the living room.

"How you do that?" he asked.

"Like this," Punky Rose said, demonstrating, taking big strides and slightly swaying back and forth with each step. "that's how they had to walk on the rolling deck of a ship," she said. "That's swashbuckling."

"Yeah, O.K.," Sheldon said, straining to imitate Punky Rose. But he just looked stupid, and because he was wearing his father's rubber fishing boots, which were about three inches too big, he stumbled instead of swashbuckling.

"I guess you'd better walk normal," Punky Rose decided.

"My mom put lots of Kleenex down these boots," Sheldon said rather dismayed, "seems they're still too big. I feel like I'm about to fall down."

"Well, don't do that," Punky Rose laughed. "I'd hate to have to pick you up and carry you around all night."

Both kids slogged out to Aunt Haz's car with their heads turned half sideways so they could see with their one good eye, the other being covered with the patch. Aunt Haz drove them the few blocks to the side of the door of the Methodist Church Social Hall and told them to have fun. They were to give her a call from the pay phone when they wanted to come home. Punky Rose just nodded and then winked at Sheldon with her unpatched eye.

They entered the church hall and gazed around at the decorations on which the Ladies Aid group had worked all afternoon. Black and orange crepe paper streamers hung from the ceiling. Big shocks of derived corn and bales of hay stood against the walls, and someone had fashioned cats and witches on pieces of newspaper print with black tempura paint. These were taped to the walls between the bales and shocks. The lights were off, and a few old-fashioned lanterns sat on the small tables used for coffee on Sundays, making the room dim and spooky. A few white-sheeted ghosts dangled from the opposite doorframe.

"This really looks dumb," Punky Rose said to Sheldon. The choir kids were arriving in droves now, princesses and cowgirls, cowboys and about twenty other pirates. "Let's go sit over there," Punky Rose said to Sheldon, pointing to some chairs by a bale. Kids giggled and someone put scary music on the record player. It sounded like the kind of music that they played on the Green Hornet radio show before the story got started.

"Now, children," Mr. Denby said, emerging from one of the side doors in a clown outfit, "there are four special attractions tonight. Over to the left is a tub where you can bob for apples. If you get five apples, you get a prize, and over to this side," he said, pointing right, "you have to put on a mask and feel some stuff and see if you can figure out what it is. It could be guts and buckets of eyeballs from the grave! And then in the cloakroom, there's a witch telling the story of the Headless Horseman, a short version of course. In the kitchen, there's another ghoulish event." He tried to say this in a frightening voice, but somehow the sight of him in the big plaid suit, wearing a bright red, rubber nose, just made Punky Rose and Sheldon laugh. "Well, let's get started," Mr. Denby continued. "Sopranos to the left, altos to the right, tenors to the cloakroom, and second tenors to the kitchen."

"Come on," Punky Rose said to Sheldon, going to the alto side of the room.

"Shouldn't I be a tenor?" Sheldon asked.

"Stick with me," Punky Rose said. "I think we should slide out of the side door and go down to the park. This kiddy party is really dumb."

"Good idea," said Sheldon, "but they've got donuts and cider on that table over there. Couldn't we do just one activity then have some lunch?"

"Yeah, sure," Punky Rose said. "Let's go feel the cold, cooked spaghetti that's supposed to be guts and the peeled grapes that's supposed to be eyeballs and get it over with." The kids got into line, and went through the ritual, even oohing and ahhing for effect until Mrs. Wenthworth Harding told Punky Rose to cut it out. Then they moseyed over to the refreshment table and scooped up some donuts and paper cups of cider. "Now," said Punky Rose. "But walk slow."

"Can't walk any other way," Sheldon said, as he followed her. They go to the door, opened it up, and walked right through it. Nobody even looked up as they left.

"Now, let's get these stupid patches off," Punky Rose said, and she and Sheldon ripped off the taped-on patches. They walked slowly down to the park several blocks away, found the swings, and sat down to munch donuts and slurp cider.

"Boy, I'll bet the little kids that trick or treat are scarfing up the candy, tonight," Sheldon said. "My mom has the biggest bowl of Tootsie Rolls you've ever seen. She said that last year almost a hundred kids came to the door."

"It's all those dumb farm kids who come into town to score," Punky Rose said. "That's what Aunt Haz says."

"Did you ever go trick or treating when you were a little kid?" Sheldon wanted to know. "I used to go with my brothers and sisters and get a whole bag full of candy."

"Nah," Punky Rose said, "My momma said the whole thing was dumb, and all that candy would rot my teeth. We turned out the lights so no one would think that we were home on Halloween. I don't get what Halloween is all about, anyway. It's dumb if you ask me."

"It's about keeping the evil spirits away," Sheldon said. "That's what my mom told us. I think it's Irish, like us McNamaras. The Irish on Samhain…"

"On what?" interrupted Punky Rose.

"On Samhain, that the Irish word, well, they lit bonfires to keep the bad spirts in hell or something like that. The only night of the year when the spirits could get you was Samhain night. But if you kept the fires going, they was afraid, see, and they'd leave you alone. After St. Patrick same, he changed Samhain to All Hallows Eve, and some dumb American called Halloween cuz they can't talk as good as the Irish, and here we are today."

"Well, you're just a fountain of knowledge, Sheldon McNamara," Punky Rose said. "You'll make a good history teacher someday." Sheldon took another bite of donut and licked the sugar from his fingers. "But there's one thing I don't get," said Punky Rose. "We had a lot of evil last summer. The spirits didn't wait for Halloween to come in Iowa, did they?"

"Yeah," said Sheldon softly. "They got us good last summer." Both kids sat swinging slightly for a while, and then Punky Rose said, "Let's brighten up Sheldon. What could we do for fun tonight?"

"I dunno," Sheldon said. "It's awful dark. What can we do in the dark?"

"I'll tell ya what, matey," a horribly gruff voice said from the direction of the bandstand. Both kids jumped about a mile into the air. The gruff voice laughed for real now. "I got you two good," he said.

Punky Rose stood up and took several steps toward the bandstand, fist clenched. Into a shaft of moonlight, Jake Barnside stepped toward her. "You horse's ass, Jake

Barnside," Punky Rose sputtered. "You could have given someone a heart attack or something." Sheldon lurched up beside her.

"Yeah? So what," Jake said back. "Two kids found dead in Ravenswood Park. No sign of a struggle. Can't you just see the headlines? Come on troops! What are you doing out here dressed up in those outfits? What are you suppose to be? Old farmers let out of the old people's home for the night?"

"We're pirates," Sheldon said coldly. "Pirates."

"O.K. you're pirates," Jake said shrugging his shoulders.

"And what are you doing out here," Punky Rose wanted to know, hands on her hips. "Shouldn't you be at one of those fancy high school parties or something, the ones where they plan Spin the Bottle?"

"Nah," Jake said, "too many of the girls would want to kiss me." He laughed to himself while Punky Rose glowered at him, and her heart beat harder when he said the word "kiss."

Back at the party, everything seemed to go wrong. Over at the bobbing-for-apples tub, Tommy Tooter gulped a mouthful of water, coughed, and water sprayed out his nose. Then he started to gag and finally puked into the tub. That made all the kids standing around him start gagging and lurching toward the restrooms. Over at the spaghetti and grapes table, Betty Frison, six-years-old, got so scared over being blindfolded and feeling about in the bowl of eyeballs, that she began to wail and wet her pants. Mary Crabtree knocked over a lantern, which fell across a bale of hay, setting it on fire. Mrs. Wentworth Harding saw the tiny flames and threw the pot of cold, wet spaghetti on it just as Mr. Denby, also seeing the flames, grabbed the fire extinguisher and raced across the hall, slipping in the spaghetti, and skidding another ten feet before he fell in a heap and the fire extinguisher rolled across the floor, tripping Penny Sardusky who splatted onto the floor and yelped.

Kids began going crazy in the chaos, running around, leaping up to catch the dangling black and orange crepe paper streamers and pulling them down. The more they jumped and yelled, the more other kids joined them. Finally Mrs. Wentworth Harding, a former gym teacher who always carried a whistle, blew into the silver nugget, making a harsh, shrill sound. She about blew her brains out in six big blows, and finally, most of the kids came to a standstill and looked in her direction. In the melee, the donut table had been knocked over and sticky smashed donuts and crushed cups of cider littered the floor. Another lady switch on the overhead lights and almost wished she hadn't when she saw the mess. "Oh my heavens," Mr. Denby cried, trying to get to his feet, cold spaghetti dangling from his big red nose. "Oh, this is awful," he moaned.

But Mrs. Wentworth Harding sprang into action. "First through third graders over against this wall," she demanded, "and fourth through sixth, over there," she pointed in the opposite direction. Kids got confused and headed for one side of the room only to realize that they were going the wrong way, and turning around, bumped into other kids doing the same. TWEET, TWEET, TWEET, sounded out across the social hall as Mrs. Wentworth Harding blew her whistle again. Kids stopped in their tracks looking around.

"I said first through third graders over here," she yelled out. Frightened little kids made the correct wall, "and all the others go to that wall," she said, changing directions. Kids obediently trudged through the goop on the floor to their assigned wall.

"Now, junior higher (and there were only about six left), to the janitor's closet and get the mops and pails. We have to clean up this mess. Mr. Denby, spray down that bale so it can't spark up again. Ladies, team A, dump that apple tub in the alley. Fourth graders only, walk forward, picking up paper products in your path and bring it over to the trash cans by the door." Kids and ladies sprang into work while Mr. Denby sprayed the bale of straw and dismally walked back to his office where he dumped the fire extinguisher into a chair, took off his red nose, and slumped into his desk chair.

Parents began arriving a half hour later to pick up their children, only to see them lined up against the wall, or cleaning up trash, or mopping through sticky puddles of cider and donuts. "My gosh, what a mess,"

Lilly Musgrave said, searching the wall for her first grader. "What happened?" Shirley Cared asked Mrs. Wentworth Harding.

"Well, if you ask me," Mrs. Wentworth Harding said peevishly, "one could have figured something like this might happen. I'm against these events altogether, you know. Halloween is a devil's night, and here is the evidence." And with that she haughtily walked towards the janitor's closet to supervise the rinsing of the mops.

Jake, Punky Rose, and Sheldon sat silently on the swings for a while. Just as Punky Rose thought of something to say, Sheldon elbowed her in the ribs and nodded at something to their left. Two cars had pulled up into the parking lot, and two men got out and walked to the bandstand. They didn't see the kids in the dark, and the three kids almost held their breaths and became as silent as rocks. They strained to hear what the men said.

All they could hear were low voices for a few moments, and then the voices raised the volume as the men began to argue. "you gonna find the money?" one voice yelled. "You gonna find it or are you gonna leave me high and dry this time just like he did?"

"I dunno what you mean," the other voice yelled back. "It was you that went out there with the gun. Wasn't me. It's you that made a mess of things. It was you who didn't find out what we came for."

"Well, you gotta plan this time, Einstein?" the other voice demanded.

"Yeah," the second voice said. "He had a wife, didn't he?"

"O.K., so what?"

"So, men tell their wives where they put things. I'll bet that girlie knows plenty."

"There's only one problem," the first voice said in a disgusted manner. "You know she's locked up tight in that looney bin. How are you gonna get to her, anyway?"

"I dunno, but I'm gonna find out how to get to her, maybe talk to that kid of hers," and he chuckled.

With that, the men's voices got quieter again, and then they walked to their cars and pulled out of the parking lot, one turning left at the stop sign, and one right. The kids watched the taillights getting dimmer and dimmer before Sheldon turned to Punky Rose. "They was talking about you and your momma," he said in a frightened voice.

Punky Rose's voice seemed frozen. She tried to reply but couldn't. "Never you mind," Jake said slowly. "Me and Sheldon's gonna take care of you. We're gonna be with you all the time."

"Yeah," whispered Sheldon. "Don't go anywhere alone. Stick with us," and all of a sudden Sheldon McNamara felt ten-feet tall.

"Think you'd better tell your Aunt Haz about this," Jake said matter-of-factly. "She'll probably want to call the sheriff. Now let me walk you two home," and the kids stood up from their swings and headed home. As they left the park, Jake Barnside slipped his hand into Punky Rose's. Sheldon pretended not to notice.

Aunt Haz couldn't get over the kids showing up at her house just about the time she expected to get a phone call. Punky Rose introduced her to Jake Barnside, who retreated once the kids were safe inside her house. "Why did you leave the party," Aunt Haz asked. "Didn't you have a good time?"

"It was dumb," Punky Rose said.

"Real dumb," Sheldon echoed. "Guess I'll go home now," he added. "You got a flashlight I could use?"

"Right on the window sill by the back door," Aunt Haz said, waving toward the kitchen. Sheldon fought the light, said good night to Aunt Haz and Punky Rose, and left by the front door.

"Punky Rose, I don't want you walking around at night with Sheldon or the Jake boy or anybody, you hear me?" Aunt Haz said with a worried voice.

"I hear ya," Punky Rose said tiredly as she headed up the stairs to her bedroom. She decided not to tell her aunt anything, not yet anyway. It had been a strange night, wearing costumes and going to the dumb party, finding Jake in the park, and then listening to strange men talk about her and her momma. What money were they looking for anyway, and were they talking about the man on the trail when they mentioned the gun and making a "mess" of things? But the event that wouldn't leave her imagination, as she tossed and turned, was that Jake Barnside had taken hold of her hand and held it tightly as they walked home. And she liked it, really liked it.

# Chapter 22

Ted Warner applied for a job as a patient orderly at the hospital where Punky Rose's mother slept away her days. The job was burnout for most people, and the hospital always needed help. Ted Warner was tall and lanky, well-muscled, clean, and had his long, hippy hair tied back in a ponytail. Now, he sat across the desk from the personnel manager, Mrs. Fratt. "You ever work in a place like this before?" she asked, narrowing her eyes at him after scanning the application. People usually lied on these applications. She didn't even bother to check their references anymore. They were always made up.

"Well, yes ma'am," Ted said with a southern drawl. "I sure did, down in Florida. Worked at a hospital just like this one."

"And why are you in Iowa?" Mrs. Fratt asked tiredly.

"Well, I came home to be with my mother. She's getting on, you know. But after a few weeks, my sister packed her up and took her to Chicago, and now I'm kinda stuck, if you know what I mean."

Another lie, Mrs. Fratt thought. No Iowa boy, even if he did live in Florida for a while, would have an accent like this one. But what did it matter. Was he running away from the bill collector? Was he following some woman here in town? Was he getting away from some small town sheriff for a series of misdemeanors? What did it matter? He looked trainable and strong, and that's what she needed, a strong young man to handle the most difficult cases, making sure that they didn't hurt themselves or anybody else. "Well, you will have to start on the night shift. Training will take a week. The pay is three hundred fifty dollars a month. Take it or leave it."

"Oh, ma'am, I'll surely take it," Ted grinned. "And I don't care about no night shift. I'm a night owl myself mostly."

"Well, that's just great," Mrs. Fratt said. "Now go down to the payroll office and fill out their forms. Training will begin tomorrow at eight am. Check in with me and don't be late."

"No ma'am," Ted said, standing up and extending his hand to her.

The night shift was exactly what Ted Warner was hoping he would get. His plan was to find Selma Bagley and see if he could get any information out of her, information that would please his partner, Rook Wilder.

Ted Warner really didn't care about the money anymore. He just wanted Wilder out of his life for good.

Ted, Rook, and Jackson had met several years ago, and the three of them had made a killing selling cocaine on the streets of Miami. But things got hot, and they decided to lay low for awhile. They divided their loot, but somehow Bagley snookered them out of about one hundred thousand dollars. Rook wanted his money. According to Bagley's landlady, he had lit out for Iowa, Ravenswood to be exact, where he had a wife and child. So, the boys packed their bags and made their way separately to Ravenswood.

They settled into a cheap motel in Fort Henry and began hanging out at the Blue Bomber Bar, just the kind of place where a guy like Bagley, a small time hustler, might be. A few people remembered him, but nobody had seen him for years.

When Jackson Bagley had arrived in town, keeping a very low profile, he'd learned all about Selma from some of his previous cronies. Someone else now lived in the house they had shared. And he had no idea where Selma's things were. He knew that the kid was living with her aunt or something. He really wanted to know where Selma's things were because before he had left Florida, he'd mailed her a shoebox all wrapped with duct tape in which he'd placed the money with a note telling her to keep her mouth shut, hide the money, and he'd contact her soon. Perhaps they could begin again in another town.

But what he didn't know, of course, was that Selma's mind was already tilting badly when she received the box. She had been thinking of other things and wasn't even curious about it. She'd tossed it in her closet and then began trying on dresses to see which one she fancied for her date that night with Yip Jenson.

Jackson spent his last few dollars at a rooming house in Fort Henry. There didn't seem to be anything more that he could do. And so on a particular August night, he decided to stop at the Blue Bomber for a beer, see if he could cheat a few farm boys at a hand of cards for a little get-away money, and hitchhike out of town, going where, he had no idea.

When Jackson saw the boys, he froze, but Rook Wilder was up in a flash, took his arm in a tight grip, and propelled him out the side door and into the alley. He told him that he would kill him if he didn't return his money, and Jackson Bagley, never one to be a hero, stalled for time, telling him that he'd meet him on the Indian Trail that ran along the river in Ravenswood. There was a big oak about twenty minutes down the trail. That's where he'd wait for him. And Rick Wilder agreed, but he told him that if he didn't show up he was a dead man absolutely.

Jackson Bagley was frightened for his life because he knew that Rick Wilder meant business. The only thing that he could think to do was try to talk him into helping him find Selma's things, Selma's kid, and the duct taped box. If he ran away this night, Wilder would just find him all over again. Wilder was cunning and never gave up. Ted Warner he could shake, but not Wilder.

Of course, nobody knew that the duct-taped box was lying in a big box behind the furnace in Aunt Haz's basement.

# Chapter 23

Jackson Bagley couldn't get away, and he couldn't figure out where the money was. He'd heard the talk in the Blue Bomber about Selma, going nuts after he left town and being packed off to Cherokee Hospital. He didn't hear much about Punky Rose. He wondered sometimes if she looked like Selma or him. But he didn't stay with that thought for long. One thing he did know. There was no talk about the woman having a shoebox of one thousand dollar bills when she was taken away. Selma might have burned the box and everything in it, for all he knew.

In fact, that'd make a good story. A story that he could tell Rook Wilder out on the Indian Trail. Hell, they'd both been snookered by a woman, goddamn. He'd suggest that they go back to Miami, get back into the game, make more money, and let bygones by bygones. It just might work. Rook had a bad temper and he'd beaten people up before, but he'd never killed anybody that Jackson knew about. And besides, none of this was his fault. It was all the fault of that bitch he'd married. He got his mind so set on the story that by the time on the hot August day that he hitchhiked up towards Ravenswood, he believed it himself. "Yessir," he'd say. "She told me she burned it in the backyard burning barrel, and then she hooted and hollered about it, and the next thing you know, her aunt drives her up to the hospital.

The long-haul trucker who picked Jackson Bagley up wished that he hadn't once the guy got into the cab. There was something creepy about him, and he was glad when, about twenty miles up the highway, just as they were approaching Ravenswood, the hitchhiker said he wanted out. He'd cut through that there cornfield and take a short cut to his brother's place. He watched the man jump the fence and disappear into the tall, green corn, and he put his rig in gear and drove on toward Omaha. It wasn't until he pulled into a truck park for the night that he saw there was something left on the hitchhiker's seat. A wallet. "Shit," the trucker said to himself, and he picked it up and put it in the glove compartment.

Jackson Bagley walked down the Indian Trail, sweat making his shirt stick to him. He wore black slacks, a white shirt, and dress shoes. It was important he not look like a bum. He'd shaved and slicked back his hair, and when he got to the old oak tree and found no one, he thought his luck had changed. He stood there for a while, just looking at the river, when a voice yelled out from above him in the tree branches. "You got it?" Jackson Bagley turned and looked up, smiled, and spread his arms out.

"No, I ain't got it, but I got a story you won't believe." But he never got to tell his story because Rook Wilder fired a pistol, hitting his mark, Jackson Bagley's forehead. Bagley fell backwards and lay still.

Rook Wilder looked closely up and down the trail. He scooped off each shoe with a free hand, stashed them inside his shirt, and descended from the tree. He took two big steps across the trail, making a kind of squishy dance step, which wiped out his tracks as he moved toward the riverbank. He nimbly stepped into the water, testing the coldness and current, and then he lay down in it and with long strokes swam to the other side. He got out of the water, threw the gun into the middle of the river, and disappeared into a cornfield on the other side. Rook Wilder was gone, and even the sheriff with his sharp eyes couldn't see any disturbance around the murdered man lying on the Indian Trail.

On the day after the murder victim was found, the trucker who had given Jackson Bagley a lift read about it in the Omaha paper. "Shit," he said to himself as he finished the article and slurped his coffee, sitting at the Halfway Diner on Highway 80. He knew what he would have to do, and so after finishing his coffee, he got into his truck and drove back toward Iowa, crossing the Missouri

River. He opened his window and threw the wallet out. It spiraled a good arc, sailing through the girders and splashing down into the water below. Two motorists saw the trucker throw something into the river, but they drove on, not thinking too much about it.

# Chapter 24

Ted Warner showed up at the hospital right on time the next morning, and he went through his one week of training. The staff taught him how to see trouble before it happened, how to tell when one of the patients was about to "go off," and how to restrain that person. "It ain't hard on the night shift," one man told him, "they's all drugged up for the night. They sleep like babies."

On his first night shift, Ted checked the nurse's roster and found out where the Bagley woman's room was. She shared it with four other patients, mostly old women with severe dementia. Nurse Norma Hadley supervised the night shift, and she liked it that way. She was a big, fat woman, immense-looking in her scrubs, and she liked to sit at the desk, snack on potato chips and cokes, and smoke cigarettes throughout the night. She never had to move very far or very fast, and she could read romance novels after the rest of the shift went home. She was the only person on the ward besides this newcomer. She made small talk with him for a few minutes before returning to her novel. She told him to go into the day room and watch TV or take a nap. She'd ring a bell if she needed him to help with anything. Nothing much ever happened on the night shift. It was easy duty.

Ted Warner smiled and walked toward the day room. He went in and turned on the TV before scooting down another hallway straight to room 704 where Selma Bagley slept a drug-induced sleep. Ted tipped the door open quietly. There were five beds, and he tread softly, stopping at each to look down at the patient. All old women, yesiree, just lying there snoring away. But the one over by the window was the one he was looking for, and he padded beside the bed and looked down at the young, blonde woman laying on her back, lips slightly open, breathing softly. That was Selma Bagley, all right. He'd seen her picture in her file. Pretty thing, really. Just a shame, she was rotting in this place. He wondered if Jackson Bagley knew anything about what had happened to her, if he'd ever come here to see her. And then as he stood there staring down at her, he got a twitching and tightening feeling in his groin and began to breathe a little ragged. Nobody would know. Hell, she probably would even wake up. He could do it, and be back out in the day room before that fat bitch nurse ever checked.

He pulled back the bedcovers. The woman's night gown was up around her hips. He moved her legs apart, and the woman sighed once, twice, and turned her head toward the window, never opening her eyes. And then Ted Warner pulled down his scrubs and underwear, climbed onto Selma Bagley, and began a rhythmic humping that felt so good. Then, Bam! it was over, and he carefully crawled off the bed, slid his pants back up, and silently left the room.

Night after night, Ted Warner visited Selma Bagley's room, sliding between her legs, kissing her neck and ear lobes. And as the silent woman lay under him, he began to feel safe with her, and warm, and even a little bit in love. Some nights, the woman seemed to emerge from her deep fog and respond to his thrusts, moaning a little herself as the old women in the room slept on. And some nights, Ted Warner found that he wanted to just lie beside her and turn her into himself where he could nuzzle her breasts and neck, kiss her lightly on the lips, and run his hands over her thighs. Some nights he didn't even turn his body into hers at all. And more and more the woman, through some deep instinct, put her arms around his chest and moved into a deep pleasurable rhythm with him. Some nights, she said, "Ooh, baby," over and over again, softly against his cheek.

And the fat nurse read about romance and chomped away at her potato chips, while the real thing was happening in room 704 right down the hall.

# Chapter 25

The day that Ted Warner had read about the murder on the Indian Trail in the Ravenswood Gazette, he had hightailed it out of Fort Henry. Rook Wilder was nowhere to be seen, and Ted never could figure out how Rook had trailed him to the next town down the road. But every few days, he received phone calls from Wilder checking in but not revealing where he was. Then he had suggested the meeting in the park in Ravenswood. That's when Ted had put him off with his new plan. Ted got this eerie feeling that he needed to disappear. He needed to go someplace where Wilder couldn't find him just to be on the safe side. He didn't care about the money anymore. He just wanted to be free of Wilder. What if Wilder got it into his head that Ted had found the money and was hiding the truth? What might he do? He needed to get out of town. But first he'd try for the job at Cherokee

Hospital. Maybe he'd find out where the money was, tell Wilder, and get him off his back.

Now the trouble was that Ted Warner had fallen in love with Selma Bagley. He came early and watched her on the day shift. He tried to talk to her, but her blank eyes didn't hold much promise of conversation. He read her file. He tried to talk to the other orderlies about her. "Selma?" Claude Peters said, "oh, she's a hellion if you don't keep her drugged. Yells and carries on, sings and goes for the throat of the nurses if they so much as touch her. Yeah, she can be a hellion, all right."

"But do you think that she's crazy? Do you think she really needs to be here?" Ted asked.

"What do I know about any of these folks?" Claude sighed. "You'd have to ask Dr. Swanson about Selma Bagley." And Ted determined that he was going to do just that.

About a week later, he saw his chance. Dr. Swanson was making his rounds and Ted caught up with him walking through the day room. "Say, Doc," he began, "I was wondering about several of the patients, kinda like."

"You're on the night shift, aren't you?" Dr. Swanson asked. "What are you doing here in the afternoon?"

"Well, I'm real interested in what makes people tick, you know? And I'm thinking maybe I'll go back to school and get to be a nurse or something. I like to study these people. Now, you take that Selma lady over there. What's really wrong with her?"

Dr. Swanson looked across the room toward where Selma sat with her head drooped down. "That's a sad one," he said. "Has delusions of being the Queen of the May, or something. Has delusions that every man in the world is in love with her. And then if her boyfriends let her down, and they all have seemed to do just that, she goes into rages that are pretty bad. Can't think straight at all. Gets into a real bad depression one minute, and rage the next. Such a shame for a young, pretty woman like Selma. But we haven't seemed to find a med that really keeps her balanced. I don't like to see her the way she is now. Way too drugged. I need to consult with the state guy, Dr. Waverly, about her." And he turned toward the door.

Ted Warner looked at Selma and wished that he could get her out of here. He already had a plan for himself. Now he wanted to include Selma. Sneak her out of the hospital at night, get so far away from Cherokee and Ravenswood that no one would ever find them. He would take her to Gualala on the Northern California coast. A motel, a run-down hotel serving good Italian food, a hamburger joint overlooking the ocean, and a straggle of old logging shacks going up the side of a hill. Rent was cheap and you could grow enough Mendocino Gold up in those hills to pay the rent and buy groceries at the Point Arena store. Yeah, that was the perfect place to escape.

He began working his plan by cutting the meds given to Selma. He practiced Dr. Swanson's handwriting carefully, and wrote in new orders on her chart. Then during his nocturnal visits, he began telling Selma that he was going to take her away.

He wondered about that kid of hers. He'd stalked her for a few days after the murder, even donned his black raincoat an skulked around the Methodist Church, but the kid's aunt kept too close to her. And another thing that Ted hadn't figured out was that nobody identified the body found on the Indian Trail. If that kid and her friend had found the body why couldn't she identify her own father? Maybe the kid had never known him?

After a week. Selma seemed to understand what he was saying, and she would spend her days, docile, and waiting for her beautiful lover to appear at night just like in the fairy tale. She didn't know where Gualala was or how they were going to get there, but it seemed that Ted Warner would take care of her, and that's all she cared about. Didn't she always get a man in the end? That old Yip Jenson! Who could care about him now? And what if Jackson Bagley came back for her and found her gone. It served him right. During the day, she began putting the pills the nurse gave her under her tongue until the coast was clear then flushing them down the toilet as Ted had told her to do. Soon Ted would take her away. Soon, he would take her away.

Jake Barnside began taking an interest in Punky Rose and Sheldon after what he heard in the park on Halloween Night. He was a boy with a man's sense of responsibility toward his family. He'd spent years taking care of his little sisters in Stockton, California, and it made him rightly sad when his mother decided to shift him off to Ravenswood and his Aunt Theresa. She told him that Theresa had agreed to pay the expenses of raising him his last two years in high school, but Jake knew it was because of his mother's new boyfriend that found in Jake a rival. Jake needed to "father" somebody, and here was Punky Rose and Sheldon.

He'd read the story of the murder on the Indian Trail like everybody else in town. He'd heard stories about the black hooded creep in the church. And now there was this new element, two men plotting something that night involving Punky Rose. He'd just keep an eye out for these kids, maybe ride his bike out to Lake Youcantoo with them for a wienie roast, get to know them. Sheldon was actually interesting to talk to, smart as a whip, with knowledge about just about everything. He read all the time. That's how Jake figured it. And that girl. That Punky Rose. She was a smart ass, clever, funny, but there was something else that he picked up. It was as if she guarded everything that she said, never revealing too much about what she was feeling. There was a depth to her, unlike his mother or Aunt Theresa. She was not just a simple girl. She was complicated. That was the word, complicated.

And so about every day when work was finished at the Creamery, he biked to the south part of town to knock on Aunt Haz's back door and say "hey" to Punky Rose. Most of the time Sheldon was there doing homework, but if he wasn't, Jake would stop by Sheldon's too.

"That Jake's a nice boy," Aunt Haz ventured after several weeks of his visits. "His mother sure must miss him. I wonder why she sent him back here. You think she'd want nothing to do with this town even if her sister still lives here."

"Why?" Punky asked her, frowning.

"Because of what Yip Jenson did to her," Aunt Haz said trailing off because she'd said too much, and now she'd have to tell Jake's mother's story.

"Yip Jenson? What's he got to do with Jake?" Punky asked.

"Well, Jake's mother, Laura, had Jake a few months after she got married, if you know what I mean. She ups and marries Yip Jenson. She has two more babies, one right after the other, and then that old Yip gets rid of her, just ships her and her children off on a bus for California. I always thought he was one of the meanest men in Ravenswood, Iowa. Laura was a nice girl. Came from a poor family, and got caught in the family way, but that happens to lots of girls. You pay attention to that Punky Rose Bagley. It can ruin a girl's life, it can."

Punky Rose went up to her room, and sat down to write in the journal she'd been keeping all school year. She began to connect the dots between the new boy's arrival in town and Yip Jenson's car being found in the gravel pit, and she smiled with satisfaction. Ole Yip Jenson deserved any bad luck that came his way. And Jake seemed to be connected to that bad luck. She couldn't wait to tell Sheldon all about it.

# Chapter 26

"Clothes! What should they wear to the McNamara's for Thanksgiving," Aunt Haz wondered.

Aunt Haz had found out through trial and error that if she discussed "clothes" with Punky Rose, she got nowhere. The girl stubbornly refused to give up her ragbag appearance. She wore it as if it was a badge of honor, making her different from everybody else. Why? Was it some kind of statement about her relationship with her mother, who got all floosied up spending what little money she had on catalog selections from scandalous designers in Chicago and Kansas City? Was it because Selma refused to spend money on her, just picking a few things up from the Salvation Army Store, that instead of feeling ashamed of her clothes, Punky Rose belligerently wore them with pride?

But Aunt Haz began to order cotton underwear from the Penney's Catalogue folding the items neatly and putting them in Punky's drawers without saying a word. She exchanged them for the ragged pairs of panties, and threw the latter into the burning barrel. One day, a training bra turned up in the drawer. Another time, there was a pair of summer pajamas and some flannel nightgowns, too. Good quality socks began appearing. Aunt Haz held her breath after every exchange, but Punky said nothing. Aunt Haz figured if she could change Punky's inside clothes, perhaps the time would come when she could change the outside too.

And there was the matter of the red wool coat and punky's tears. That was the only time that there had been words or a break through. Now, Thanksgiving was coming, and the McNamaras had invited Aunt Haz and Punky to join them for dinner. Aunt Haz wanted Punky to look "nice" for a change. So, the night before the big event, she laid out a plaid blue and white wool pleated skirt and matching blue fuzzy sweater on Punky's bed.

"What's this?" Punky said coming down the stairs with the new clothes in her hands.

"Oh just something to wear for Thanksgiving dinner," Aunt Haz said casually as if she had no investment in the matter. "Why don't you try it on?" She turned from where the girl stood and got busy making the pie she was taking to the McNamaras.

"What's wrong with my jeans and a sweatshirt?" Punky asked snottily.

"Oh nothing," Aunt Haz said, "Wear what you like," and she went on with her pie making.

But the next morning after breakfast and chores, Punky donned the new outfit, and Aunt Haz saw her appraising herself in her mirror. "Punky Rose? Go down to the basement and get me one of those peach lug boxes, would ja? I have to carry this pie in something sturdy," she called out to her. Punky went to the basement and brought up the box. "Thanks, honey," Aunt Haz said turning slightly away from the counter catching a look at the girl. "Well," she said smiling and turning all the way toward her, "that looks real nice, Punky, real nice."

"Don't think I'll wear it," Punky said matter-of-factly.

"Well, as you please," Haz said and got busy again.

But an hour later when they headed for the car, Punky was still wearing the new skirt and sweater.

# Chapter 27

The frost was on the pumpkin in Ravenswood, Iowa, and on everything else too, as Thanksgiving loomed. Mrs. McNamara had invited Aunt Haz, Punky Rose, and Theresa and Jake Barnside to have dinner with her family. Aunt Haz was delighted. She really liked the McNamaras, and the invitation meant that she wouldn't have to cook dinner nor would she have to make the obligatory trip to Cherokee. She'd send a card to Selma to say they'd visit the next weekend. Of course, Selma probably wouldn't know the difference, bu the staff would when they read her letter. And that was important to Aunt Haz.

Punky Rose felt a little odd as she approached the McNamara's front door.

"My gosh," Sheldon said when he opened the door to Aunt Haz and Punky Rose. "My big bubble gosh!" Punky Rose smiled slightly and shrugged, as if her new look was nothing big, and then she scanned the living room for Jake Barnside.

"Why, Miss Punky Rose Bagley," Mrs. McNamara said. "Don't you look like heaven itself. Welcome Haz. What you go there? One of those cranberry and orange slice pies that everyone talks about? You come right on in here." She ushered Aunt Haz into the kitchen.

Punky Rose went to the window seat and sat down. "You sure don't look like Rag Bagley today," Sheldon said, warming up to her new look. He sat down beside her. All the other McNamaras had looked up briefly at her entrance and then turned their attentions back to the football game on TV. Now they yelled as somebody made a touchdown. Punky Rose and Sheldon never watched football games with the rest of the family. They had long ago decided that the games were fake.

They looked at their hands, now strangely shy with each other for the first time ever, and then Sheldon squinted his eyes at Punky Rose. "Oh, I get it," he said softly so that only she could hear. "Jake Barnside is coming for dinner. That's it. You're all dressed for Jake Barnside."

"Oh, rat's ass," Punky shot back at him. "Aunt Haz said I had to come like this. It wasn't my idea."

"I'll be if Jake Barnside wasn't coming to dinner, you'd be wearing them old jeans and the Mickey Mouse T-shirt, for damn sure," Sheldon countered.

"Oh shut up, Sheldon," Punky demanded.

"Gonna make me?" Sheldon shot back.

Punky Rose clenched her fist just as there was a knock on the door, and Mrs. McNamara came out of the kitchen to open it. Punky Rose and Sheldon seethed in their places. Jake Barnside and his aunt stepped inside. She carried a covered dish. "Green bean and bacon casserole." The little woman handed the dish over to Mrs. McNamara.

"Well, welcome," Mrs. McNamara said. "Family," she said, "this here's Theresa and Jake Barnside," and all of the McNamaras turned their heads toward the guests and waved them into the living room.

"Sit down and watch this here game," Mr. McNamara said. "It's a good 'un." Theresa smiled, but turned toward the kitchen. Jake sat down on the couch, ignoring Punky Rose and Sheldon who still sat on the window seat. Before long he was hooting and hollering with all the rest of the McNamaras. Punky Rose felt absolutely stupid, and Sheldon's face was red and his jaw was clenched.

In half an hour, Mrs. McNamara called everyone to the table for the feast. Sheldon took his time getting to the table, and Punky Rose sulked as she sat next to her aunt. Jake Barnside watched her across the table, observing something very wrong with Sheldon and Punky Rose. "Let's say our prayers," Mr. McNamara said. Everyone bowed their heads and he began. "Bless us, O Lord, and these thy gifts which we are about to receive from the bounty of our Lord, Jesus Christ." The McNamaras crossed themselves, and the others looked up and smiled.

Dishes and platters were passed around the table, and everyone seemed to be laughing and talking at the same time. Aunt Haz noticed Sheldon pushing his food around on his plate, not digging in as the rest of the clan was. "Why, Sheldon," she said, "you ain't eating the way you usually do. Don't you feel good today?"

"I'm just fine," he snapped back. His mother shot him a look that said No More Smart Mouth Out of You, and Sheldon looked down at his plate. Punky Rose ate methodically, and Jake Barnside inhaled his food.

"This is really good, Aunt Haz said, nodding at Mrs. McNamara, and everyone made agreeing noises at the hostess. Sheldon looked utterly defeated and asked to be excused. Punky Rose watched him walk forlornly up the stairs.

As the meal ended, and the women began picking up dishes returning them to the kitchen, Punky Rose went back to the window seat. The McNamaras returned to the TV, but this time Jake came to sit by her. "You better go up there and tell him that you're sorry," he said softly. "I don't know what happened, but it sure looks to me as if you two had a fight, and it's not worth it, whatever it is."

"Oh, rat's ass." Punky Rose stood up and headed toward the stairs. She knocked on Sheldon's door and went inside. "Hey," Punky Rose said softly.

"Hey," Sheldon said without looking up. He sat at his desk doodling on a piece of paper.

"Well, Squint, I'm sorry," she said.

"Oh, I shouldn't have said anything about Jake," Sheldon admitted, looking up at her. Punky Rose sat on the end of his bed.

"Well, you were right," she told him. "Aunt Haz bought me the outfit, but I wanted to look nice today, well since Jake was going to be here and all."

"What are you – in love or something?" Sheldon asked in a cranky voice.

"You can't be in love in the seventh grade," Punky retorted. "You have to be in high school, at least."

"Maybe some people do things early, like fall in love." Sheldon looked down at his drawing.

"Well, maybe," Punky Rose said, looking serious. "But, hey, Sheldon, let's go down and get us some pie and forget all about this love stuff."

"That's good by me," Sheldon said with a smile. The two children grinned at each other, and then they both rushed to see who could get to the kitchen first. Jake saw the two of them coming down the stairs smiling and pushing each other.

"Must be all right now," he thought. And that was good.

# Chapter 28

On the Saturday after Thanksgiving, Aunt Haz and Punky Rose drove to Cherokee to see Selma. Punky Rose brought a box of chocolates for her mother. While Aunt Haz went to speak with Dr. Swanson, Punky Rose settled down with her mother in the day room. Selma seemed docile today, and that was a good sign. "Momma," she looked quietly at her mother, "there's something I want to know about my father." Selma looked off to one side of Punky Rose, as if she didn't want to become engaged in the conversation.

"Do I look like him?" Punky Rose asked.

"No," said Selma.

"Well, what did he look like anyway?" Punky Rose continued.

"He was a wanderer, that's all," Selma said sadly. "Just a wanderer."

"But what did he look like, momma?" Punky Rose began again.

"Oh, he was dark, you know, black hair and eyes," Selma contributed. She continued to look at the door as if expecting someone. "Perfect, you might say," Selma said almost absent-mindedly. "Except for his little finger on his right hand. Got cut off in some accident. Down to the knuckle, cut off it was."

The hair on the back of Punky Rose's neck stood up. Black hair and the right little finger cut off... just like the man on the Indian Trail. Could that man have been Jackson Bagley, her father? But why was he on that trail, and what did he have that the men in the park wanted?

Aunt Haz joined them. She smiled at Selma, who seemed to get more vacant-eyed by the minute. "You seem good today, Selma," Aunt Haz said as she patted Selma's hands clenched together in her lap. Selma nodded and kept looking at the door. "Seems like getting this rest in this here hospital is good for you." Selma didn't react. An awkward silence followed. Aunt Haz looked around the room trying to think of something to say, but nothing much came to mind. The girl and two women sat quietly for a while, and then Aunt Haz announced that it was time for them to leave. They stood up to go, but Selma didn't move a muscle. "See you in a few weeks," Aunt Haz said. "Now Punky Rose, kiss you mother good-bye." Punky Rose stooped to kiss her mother softly on the cheek. Little did she know that this would be the last time she would ever see Selma Bagley.

Ted Warner had a plan all worked out. Several days later, he got Selma out of bed, dressed, and walked right out of the employee's entrance with Selma. He helped her into his old battered car, and they drove away slowly into the night. He had told Nurse Hadley that he felt the flu coming on and he needed to go back to his motel to lay down. She had nodded and continued reading her magazine. But the next morning when Selma didn't show up for roll call, the alarm sounded and orderlies searched the hospital and grounds for her.

Nurse Hadley called Ted's motel, finally being suspicious, and found out that he had checked out the day before. The police were called and a report was made, but nobody searched too hard for the couple, and eventually Dr. Swanson had to call Aunt Haz with the news.

Selma's get-away. That's what Aunt Haz referred to the event ever after, if it came up in conversation. And at some level, she felt relieved. She'd worried about Selma's fate from the day she had signed the papers for her to be committed. Now, she felt strangely at peace with all that had happened.

"I think my momma's better off wherever she ran," Punky Rose told Sheldon McNamara. "Maybe she'll find true love with that orderly they say she run off with," she added.

"Huh!" humphed Sheldon. "True love, whatever that is."

Punky Rose chewed on the end of one braid. "Aunt Haz said that the only thing wrong with my momma was that she was always looking for true love and never found it."

"The whole subject makes me nervous," Sheldon said. "I don't intend to ever find true love. It just gets you in trouble, that's what I see."

"But what about your momma and daddy?" Punky Rose said. "Don't you think they found true love?"

"Jeeze Louise," Sheldon exclaimed. "They're my parents. Parents aren't in love." Sheldon was adamant on that issue, so Punky Rose knew there was no reason to pursue the idea.

"You gonna tell your aunt what your momma said about YOUR DADDY?" Sheldon had an edge to his voice.

"I think I'm gonna let sleeping dogs lie like Aunt Haz says. I don't want to have to talk about it anymore with anybody. I mean, momma's gone, my daddy's gone, those men in the park are gone, leastwise we haven't seen them ever again. Maybe it's best to let it all be instead of stirring trouble up again."

"You're probably right," mused Sheldon. "It's enough that we know. It's our secret."

"That's right Squint," Punky Rose smiled at Sheldon.

"Sure enough Rag Bagley," Sheldon smiled back.

On the Monday after Thanksgiving, Mrs. Gens, the social worker, called Aunt Haz at the John Deere dealership. "Punky Rose's case came up for review," she told Aunt Haz. "I'd like to talk to you about the future." So, Aunt Haz took off work at 2:00 and met Mrs. Gens in her office.

"We have a strange situation here," she began. "On the one hand we have Punky Rose Bagley with no parents to take care of her, and you doing emergency duty. On the other hand, we don't know anything about her father or his whereabouts, and now her mother has disappeared. She might show up again. She might not. Meanwhile, we have to make permanent arrangements for the girl on the presumption that her parents are solidly out of the picture. We need to find an adoptive home for the girl. How are you feeling about her at this point?"

Aunt Haz took a long time to answer. "Well, I don't know much about raising children," she began. "I just have common sense, but that seems to work. I wasn't looking forward to taking her on, as you know, saw it as my Christian duty, and that was all. And I think that Punky Rose has had it in the back of her mind that she could get shipped somewhere else. She doesn't make up to a person easily. Oh, we get along and all, but she's wary all the time as if something awful is about to happen. And then with all that bad stuff this summer, the man on the

Indian Trail and all, I can understand why she's wary. But you know, there's something about that child that I've really taken to, wariness and all. I would hate to see her go off and live with someone else."

"So, would you be willing to become her guardian?" Mrs. Gens asked.

"Yes, I would," Aunt Haz smiled at the woman.

"Well, we would have to draft court papers to make it legal and everything. And then you can apply for social security. I think that a minor like Punky Rose would be eligible for about $250/month. If you don't have a lawyer to help draw up the papers, we have Mr. Edison who helps out in family court. He could do it for you."

"I suppose that I should discuss this with Punky Rose," Aunt Haz said. "I wouldn't want to spring it on her, our decisions without her being in on it and all."

"That's very sensitive of you," Mrs. Gens said. "Call me when you want to get started with the proceedings, and I'll relate our conversation to the review committee."

Aunt Haz drove home mulling the whole thing over in her mind. What if they did the paperwork, and Selma showed up again? If she did, most likely she'd have to go back to the hospital or to jail! Whatever happened, she never had taken care of her child. What would be different this time? No, Hazel Limestone felt committed to her great niece forever and a day, Selma or no Selma.

When Punky Rose and Sheldon arrived home after school, they were surprised to find Aunt Haz already home. "Took off a little early today," was all she said. The kids spread their homework out on the table and began to discuss their review of decimals and fractions. They finished about thirty minutes later, and Sheldon gathered up his books and papers.

"See ya tomorrow," he said going out the door just as Jake arrived. Jake stuck his head inside the door.

"Hey," he said, and then he turned back to Sheldon. "Guess what I saw come into town?"

"What?" Sheldon asked squinting at him and adjusting his glasses.

"A truck load of new Chevies. Wanna bike out to the dealership and look them over?"

"What for?" Sheldon asked.

"Oh, just to see the new models and drool over them," Jake said. Sheldon smiled at being included in this guy thing.

"Sure," he concluded. "Give me a ride home on your handle bars so I can get my bike." And with that, Sheldon and Jake left.

"Boys," Punky Rose said rather wistfully, then she turned down her mouth. "Who wants to go see new cars, anyway?"

"Probably you," Aunt Haz countered. "But I'm glad that you aren't going because I have something to discuss with you." She sat down at the yellow, Formica table.

"I had a talk with the social worker, Mrs. Gens, today," she began. Punky immediately looked down and began doodling on her math homework. "It's OK, girl," Aunt Haz said, "nothing to worry about." And then she related the conversation. Punky Rose sat absolutely still taking in every word.

"I told Mrs. Gens that I wouldn't make a decision without talking to you and seeing how you felt about our arrangement first," Aunt Haz told the girl. "So can you tell me what you think?"

"So the county could just come and take me and put me in another home somewhere?" Punky asked in a tight voice.

"Well, officially you are their responsibility," Aunt Haz said. "Our arrangement was temporary until the doctors knew what to do with your mother, but now that she's gone, and may be forever, the county wants to settle your case. Technically, you are a ward of the court. They want to change that."

"So, you'd be my new mother?" Punky asked.

"Oh, no," Aunt Haz laughed. "I can never be your mother, new or old. I'd be like your guardian, but still your great aunt. I'd be responsible for you, and I'd make all the decisions about your welfare until you're eighteen. Then you're on your own."

"But what if you get mad at me or something?" Punky Rose asked.

"What do Sheldon's parents do when they get mad at him?" Aunt Haz asked. "I'm sure they get mad at him sometimes, maybe even had a big, fat fight, but then everybody has to cool down and work things out. The McNamaras wouldn't give Sheldon away just because they got mad at him, now would they?"

"No, I guess not," Punky Rose said softly.

"So, that's the way it would be with us. If we don't agree on something, then we have to talk it out. But you have to understand that until you're eighteen, my word has to be final."

"So, you're gonna start bossing me around?" Punky Rose said with an angry face.

"Do I boss you around now?" Aunt Haz asked.

"Well, not really, but you do make me go to that dumb children's choir. I hate that."

"Hmm," said Aunt Haz. "Why don't we compromise. You know what that means?"

"Yeah," Punky Rose said.

"OK, you sing with the children's choir until the Christmas concert, and then you can quit. But you have to sing, not just pretend to sing. Agreed? That way you wouldn't be letting Mr. Denby down."

"Oh as if he cares a rat's ass whether I sing or not," Punky said with a withering look.

"Don't know what Mr. Denby's thinking," Aunt Haz said, "but I know what I'm thinking, and it wouldn't be fair to drop out right now when he needs all of the voices for the Christmas concert."

Punky Rose shrugged and looked down at her homework. "Why don't you think about it," Aunt Haz said. "It's a lot of information all of a sudden. But let's set a deadline. Two days from now, I want your answer, right after you get home from school. Is that a fair deal?"

Punky Rose just shrugged again, gathered up her things, and headed for her room. Aunt Haz sighed, put on her apron, and opened the refrigerator door scanning her provisions. She prodded the wrapped parcels in the meat drawer. Pork chops. That's what she'd fix tonight. Pork chops and mashed potatoes and some of that good frozen corn that they'd put up last summer. She busily began to prepare the meal.

Two days later, when Aunt Haz got home from work, Punky Rose met her in the kitchen. "You know that stuff we talked about?" she asked. "Well, I guess it's all right." And then she left the room before Aunt Haz could respond.

# Chapter 29

December 18th was the night of the Methodist's Christmas Concert. It began with the children's choir and finished with the adult choir. Then there was a sing-along, and finally refreshments in the social hall. Half of the town, even some Catholics showed up for the festivities. Aunt Haz had suggested that Punky Rose wear her hair loose and curled for the big event, and she should wear her new wool skirt and sweater. Punky Rose had rolled her eyes at the suggestion, but the night before the big event, she had allowed Aunt Haz to wrap her freshly washed hair into big, foam rollers. So, she arrived in the church with curly hair and a new outfit, but Mr. Denby had to spoil it all by insisting the choir wear the ratty choir robes that he'd gotten on discount somewhere. Little kids wore robes down to their ankles, and the jr. high's robes barely covered their knees. The sleeves brushed their elbows. "This looks ridiculous," Punky Rose said to Aunt

Haz, as her aunt helped her into her assigned bright red robe. "Oh, rat's ass," she declared as Aunt Haz tied a big white bow around her neck.

"Shh," Aunt Haz said looking around hoping no one had heard her niece's opinion. "It's just for tonight. You are standing in back. Nobody will see your legs or arms."

The church was darkened and filled with candle light. Poinsettias formed a hedge across the altar steps. It was snowy and cold outside, and the church's furnace had been turned on at noon. It was downright hot, and bundled-up people began to shed coats and gloves immediately as they sat down. People packed into the pews. Even Jake, his Aunt Theresa, Sheldon, and the entire McNamara clan had come to see the performance. Punky Rose spied them sitting in the fourth row to the left and felt humiliated. The minister, Mr. Halsey, welcomed everyone for coming, and the children's choir trudged to their risers, the little kids tripping over their gowns. Mr. Denby, very self importantly, stood before the choir with hands raised for attention. With a downturn, the choir began to sing O Little Town of Bethlehem, Away in a Manger, and Hark the Herald Angels Sing. Verses were hard for the little kids, so they mumbled through them, but everyone sang full voice on the choruses, and at the end of their singing, audiences clapped and clapped. Mr. Denby was in his element and took three important bows before indicating that the shuffling children should return to the choir room. "You did just great," he assured them, as a few volunteer high school girls helped the kids out of their robes and bows. Then he left quickly for the adult choir segment.

The kids were supposed to sit on the floor of the choir room and remain silent until the intermission when they could join their families, but with the excitement of the evening, that was impossible, of course. They bounced around the room, hitting each other, and playing tag while the high school girls just stood there not knowing what to do. One girl kept waving her arms at them and saying, "Shhh," as if that would calm them down. Punky Rose stood up against the wall waiting for the time that she could escape.

Finally intermission came and Punky joined her family. The adult choir came on the altar for the second time and sang parts of Handel's Messiah, the audience having a sing-along, and then everyone exited to the social hall for Christmas cake and punch. But Punky Rose and family had barely gotten seated when they heard the fire engines begin to wail, and someone rushed into the room and said that a house was on fire in the north part of town, just two blocks away. It was Ole Yip Jenson's house, and people began grabbing their coats and making their way up the street to the scene of the fire munching on Christmas cake. Punky Rose and her group joined them. The town residents stood about half a block away watching the house burn while the volunteer fire department sprayed oceans of water on the blaze. It took over an hour for the flames to be doused, and by that time, Punky Rose's feet were like blocks of ice. So were everybody else's. "Let's go home," Aunt Haz said heading back to the church's parking lot.

"That was something," Sheldon said to Punky Rose. "First Yip's car gets driven into the gravel pit, and now his house burns down." Jake Barnside said nothing.

Several days later, the Ravenswood Gazette had a front page picture of the burning house and a long article about it which said that the fire marshall after investigating said that it looked like arson. The investigation was on-going. "Arson!" Aunt Haz exclaimed. "I wonder who would want to burn that house down?"

"Probably about half the town," Punky Rose answered looking at the paper.

# Chapter 30

Sheriff Conneally had another mystery on his hands. He decided to call in that Barnsdale kid to have a talk. He knew that Yip had been married to Jake's mother, and that the car incident happened shortly after the teenager had come to town to live with his aunt. He also knew that Jake was seen with that Bagley girl and McNamara boy who seemed to be in the middle of everything bad that happened in the town, not that they had anything to do with each of the incidences, but there they were just the same. Sheriff Conneally called Jake at home and asked him to come to his office.

"Now Jake," he began. "I just want to ask you a few questions."

"Do I need a lawyer or anything?" Jake asked.

"No," Sheriff Conneally said, "unless you want one present."

"Let's just do it," Jake said.

"OK, the night of the fire, where were you?" the sheriff began.

"I was with the McNamaras, my aunt, Haz Limestone, and Punky Rose Bagley at the Christmas concert at the Methodist Church."

"What time did you go to the church?"

"I think the concert was at 7:00 so probably fifteen minutes before that."

"And where were you before that?"

"At work. I work at the Creamery. I usually get off about 5:30, but they have this run on eggnog now, and I ended up working until a little after 6:00."

"And can your boss verify that?" the sheriff continued.

"Yeah, sure," Jake said.

"I got home just in time to change my clothes and go to the church."

"Now, I know that your mother was married to Yip Jenson, and that you lived with him until you were five or six before you moved to California. Is he your father? What was that like? Can you remember anything?"

"He is not my father!" Jake said with contempt. "I can remember how much I hated him. I sure can remember that."

"Why?" the sheriff asked.

"Because he made my momma cry all the time," Jake said. "They were always fighting, and he hit her, too. I can remember that. And then one day, we just got on the bus and left."

"Why did your mother ship you back here to live with your aunt?" the sheriff asked.

"Because she had a hard time making ends meet, and I guess that I ate a lot or something. Besides, she said I could help my aunt out if I worked and gave her money to help out with my board and room."

"Now, about the time you came to town, someone drove Yip Jenson's car into the gravel pit. Did you know about that?"

"Yeah, I heard about it."

"From whom?"

"Oh, Sheldon and Punky Rose, I think."

"Here you are a high school boy, and those kids are in the 7th grade. I know the three of you hang around together. What's that story?"

"I dunno. They were the first kids I talked to in Ravenswood. And then there was Halloween and those men in the park talking about Punky Rose's mother and where some money might be. Scared her to death, and I just wanted to take care of them, I guess. Then, I met Punky's aunt and the McNamaras. They began inviting my aunt and me to things, like Thanksgiving dinner, and now it seems as if we're all family or something. I pal around with Conor McNamara, too. He's in my grade at school."

"Hmm," said the sheriff. "Let's go back to the story about Halloween night. Can you tell me more about that?"

"Well, Punky Rose and Sheldon went to the Methodist Halloween party and thought it was dumb, so they slipped out the door and went to the park. They was swinging and talking when I came up behind them and scared them."

"What were you doing in the park after dark?"

"I dunno, just riding my bike around. I didn't get invited to any parties or anything. Well, we talked for a few minutes, and then two cars pulled up, and two men got out and began talking. It seems they were trying to figure out how to get to Punky Rose's mother and Punky Rose herself, wondering if she knew anything about some money. I couldn't make it out, but it scared Sheldon and Punky Rose to death, and I walked them home after the men left."

"Well, that's an interesting story," the sheriff said. "Think I'll have to talk to Punky Rose about it. Now Jake, let me get right down to it. Did you have anything to do with Yip's car being driven into the gravel pit or the burned down house?"

"I don't know nothing about his house burning down," Jake said smiling at the sheriff.

"Um, ha, I get your meaning," the sheriff said. "Let's just say a prank happened at the gravel pit, but if I ever find out there's more to it, I'll be on you like flies on shit. You get my meaning?"

"Yessir, I do," Jake said.

"OK, go home and behave," the sheriff said standing up and going to his door to open it for Jake to exit.

Sheriff Conneally dialed Haz Limestone's number. It was Saturday and he hoped that she would be home. Punky handed the phone to Aunt Haz with a surprised look on her face. "It's the sheriff," she said.

"Oh, Lord," Aunt Haz uttered before saying hello.

"Hello, Hazel, this is Sheriff Conneally. I have a few questions to ask you and Punky Rose. You think that you could come up to the office this afternoon?"

"Why, sure," Aunt Haz said, "we could be there in thirty minutes. What's going on?"

"Oh I just have a few questions about Halloween night," he said.

Aunt Haz got off the phone. "The sheriff wants to see us, says something about Halloween night. Did something happen that night that I don't know about?"

Punky Rose's heart sank and she looked down at the floor. "Well, I guess something did."

"I'd like to know about it before we go to the sheriff's office," Aunt Haz said quietly. She went to the stove and poured herself a cup of coffee from her old percolator. "Now sit down at this table and tell me what happened," she said. Punky Rose began the story of the men in the park and Jake Barnside walking she and Sheldon home. "Hmm, I wonder if one of those galoots was the one that worked at the hospital and made off with Selma?" Aunt

Haz mused. "The hospital people said that this Ted guy had only worked there a few weeks, when he bundled Selma out of there and took off. But what would they want Selma for and what's this about money? Selma didn't have any money."

"I guess there's something else that I should tell you," Punky Rose said, sighing.

"Oh my God, now what?" Aunt Haz said in an alarmed voice.

"Well, the last time I saw momma, I asked her about my dad, and she didn't say much. Couldn't seem to concentrate. But she did say that he had beautiful hands except his little finger on his right hand had been cut off when he was a kid or something." Aunt Haz's hair on the back of her neck began to bristle.

"The man on the Indian Trail," she said softly.

"I think so," Punky Rose said.

"Well, child, you just comb your hair now, and we'll walk uptown," Aunt Haz said finishing her coffee. Punky Rose went into the bathroom to brush her hair, and Aunt Haz just sat at the table with her head in her hands.

Aunt Haz and Punky Rose walked to the sheriff's office slowly.

"Howdy, ladies," the sheriff began. "Now, Punky Rose, I was talking to Jake Barnside, and he tells me that there was a little excitement Halloween night in the park. Is that right?"

"Yeah," the girl said, looking at her lap.

"Well, tell me about it, step by step," he said.

Punky Rose began her story with the Methodist party, her venture to the park with Sheldon, Jake's frightening them, and then the men showing up having a conversation about her Momma and herself. "Then I was scared, so Jake walked us home," she concluded.

"Well, so far the story matches," the sheriff said. "What money do you think the men were talking about?"

"I don't know cuz Momma never had no money. But there's something else. The last time that I talked to Momma before she disappeared, I asked her about my dad. She was all dreamy like cuz of her medicine, I guess, but she told me that he had black hair and beautiful hands, except for his right little finger being almost cut off in an accident. That's all she said, but I just knew what that meant right away."

"And you didn't tell anyone... Aunt Haz or anybody."

"No."

"And why not?"

"I dunno. Maybe I just didn't want to think about it."

"Well, you go on home now, and relax," the sheriff said. "And if you think of any little detail about any of these events, will you please let me in on it?" The girl nodded, and Aunt Haz looked relieved.

After the woman and girl left, Sheriff Conneally bean making a chronological list of events from the car in the quarry to the latest disappearance of Selma Bagley. He circled questions in red pen. Money? The murder victim? The murderer? This Ted Sorenson guy, who took off with Selma. He'd have to put out a questionnaire to law enforcement all over the country to see if anybody knew anything about these characters.

That night Punky Rose mused about her father in her journal. She made her own list. Name: Jackson Bagley. Black hair, beautiful hands, except for the right little finger being missing. Left her momma and her when she was six months old. A drifter. She drew a line under these facts, skipped a few lines, and began to jot down questions. She had such a weird feeling about this man who had helped create her, was the most intimate part of her, if her science teacher was to be believed, yet was a stranger. And since she had grown up without him literally and conventionally with her mother, he was a phantom in her mind. He didn't exist. She didn't think about him because he didn't exist.

The phantom had returned. Why did the good Lord in Heaven direct her steps that awful day to find a man that didn't exist? Why her? If Sheldon was right and guardian angels took care of you, why did hers look the other way that hot afternoon? Or was it some sort of divine plan? She laid down her pen. Holy cats, now she was beginning to sound like those Catholic McNamaras who thought that everything in this world had something to do with God, whoever or whatever that was.

# Chapter 31

Sheriff Conneally dialed Yip Jenson's phone number in Florida. A woman's voice answered. "This here is Sheriff Conneally from Ravenswood," he said. "Mrs. Jenson?"

"No, not yet," the fairy voice said at the other end of the line.

"Well, is Yip there? I need to speak with him," the sheriff continued.

"Yip? Oh yeah, old Yip. Here somewhere. I'll have to find him, find my shoes first, might be out on the beach, or playing cards with the boys at Craft's. Might be there. But shoes. Right. Shoes. Might be outside."

"Ma'am? Are you all right?" the sheriff asked, squinting into the phone. "I mean is everything all right?"

"All right?" the voice said dreamily. Never been all right. But Yip brings home the bacon, if you know what

I'm saying. Bacon. Now them shoes," and her voice trailed away.

"Well, you just tell him to call Ravenswood, the sheriff's office, OK?"

"Yeah, sure," the voice seemed to float in the air somewhere.

"You remember now," Sheriff Conneally said, hanging up. "What bubble-headed marshmallow had Yip got himself tangled up with now?" the sheriff wondered. He knew that he'd have to call him back.

Two days later, Sheriff Conneally called back and Yip answered the phone. "Got some bad news for you," the sheriff said.

"What's that?" Yip groused.

"Two nights ago, your house caught on fire and about burned to the ground. The boys tried real hard to save it, but it had a real head start by the time they got there." There was a long silence. "Yip? Are you there?" he asked.

"Burned to the ground, you say? The garage and car too?"

"Yeah, just about everything's gone," the sheriff said.

"Well, call that rascal lawyer of mine, Mr. Twiggs, and have him get in touch with me about the insurance, Yip said.

"Sure will," Sheriff Conneally said and hung up. "Now that was a strange conversation," he thought. "Yip didn't seem surprised or upset. It wasn't the reaction of a man who'd just been told that his property was destroyed by a fire at all. He'd call Mr. Twiggs all right, and then he'd call Fire Chief Benjamin. He felt a sour stomach coming on and reached in his desk drawer for a Tums.

Yip Jenson put the phone on the hook and stared at Natalie, who lay prone on the couch. He thought for a few minutes before walking into the bedroom and pulling out a small, tin suitcase from under the bed. Natalie was zonked. He didn't have to worry about her disturbing him. He opened the suitcase and moved some envelopes out of the way. At the bottom of the suitcase lay bundled up money, packets of fifties and one hundreds. He counted out five thousand. Then he opened an envelope he'd picked up at random and looked at the photos inside, photos he'd been looking at for years, pornographic photos of young girls that always gave him a hard-on. He rubbed his crotch a few times, and then shut the suitcase and slid it back under the bed. He'd do Natalie right there on the couch. And she probably wouldn't know the difference. That's what he liked about her. Silent and zonked. It was the only way to have a woman around and keep your head together.

# Chapter 32

As things would have it, a strange connection was made in one of the seaside taverns where Yip Jenson frequented. Wilder had begun hanging out there, and he got very interested when he found out that Yip Jenson hailed from Ravenswood, Iowa. "Been there one time," he said cautiously to Yip. "Pretty little town."

"Pretty little town, for sure," was all that Yip said in return.

But before long, the men began doing business with each other, as Wilder was selling what Natalie needed and Yip supplied. And they got to talking. "Was a woman lived there," Rick said one day, named "Selma Bagley. You ever hear of her?"

"Hear of her?" Yip smirked. "I done her regular for a few months. But she was real crazy, and she ended up in the hospital at Cherokee. She was a hot one, I can tell you."

"Ever wonder about her husband, that Bagley fella?" Rick ventured. "Didn't she have a kid or something?"

"Yeah, she had a kid," Yip said. "I hate kids."

"But what about the kid's father?" Rick demanded more adamantly.

"Don't know," Yip said. "I never met him or heard anything about him. Selma never said anything about him. Hey? Whadaya want to know about him for, anyways?"

"Well, I met Jackson Bagley in Miami once," Wilder said. "He was a drifter, but he talked about a wife and kid in Ravenswood, Iowa. We did business, ya know? And then, he skipped out on me. I went to Ravenswood looking for him, but he wasn't there and nobody had seen him for years. Funny that I meet somebody else from that damned little town.

"Well, if he's a drifter, you probably won't never find him," Yip said. "Now about what I owe ya…"

It was later that night, that Yip got to thinking about Ravenswood and that old house sitting there, and then he got to thinking about his photo lab and dark room in the basement. And the more he thought about it, the more he thought it might be a good idea to make sure that nobody else ever saw it. When somebody hotwired his car and drove it into the gravel pit, he began to have the weird feeling that someone wanted revenge. But revenge for what? His shady business deals? His sporting with the town's women? But he made a point to have people over a barrel before seducing their wives or taking their money. It was a game that he played, and he played it very well. He was always sly about letting the injured party know that the stakes were way too high for them to even think about revenge. But somebody had taken that car out of his garage. And what if that somebody decided to break into the house and begin nosing around?

He didn't want to go back to Ravenswood either. What would Natalie do if he was gone for the week? There was only one thing to do, and that was to burn the whole thing to the ground, collect the insurance, and nobody would be the wiser, plus the insurance money would come in handy with Natalie's needs and all. And that's when Yip began thinking about Rick Wilder. He'd already been to Ravenswood. He'd said so. And with his habits, Yip thought he might be just the one to agree to torch the place. And if he made a mistake and got caught? Yip would play the good citizen's role, act outraged at any suggestion the crook might make to the police. Nobody would believe Rick Wilder after they checked up on his record. Yes, torch the place after bringing a couple of suitcases back. Things he didn't want found would be in cinders and the insurance money would could rolling in. It was a good plan.

The following night at the tavern, as Rick and Yip did business, Yip told him that he had a job for somebody to do in Ravenswood, and the job was worth about five thousand dollars. Was he interested? And of course,

Wilder was. He was already on the lookout for money, since his regular business hardly covered his own habits. And so, over a pitcher of beer, the two men planned the event.

Rick Wilder, driving a non-descript old gray car with Iowa license plates stolen a long time ago, drove slowly up to Iowa. This would be a simple job. But there was one thing that nagged him. The house in Ravenswood couldn't be worth much. Why did Yip Jenson want it torched? If he wasn't going back to Ravenswood, why didn't he just sell it? It didn't make sense when you really thought it through. Why was it so important to get rid of the house by having it torched? There was only one conclusion. There was something IN THAT HOUSE that the old geezer wanted destroyed. And what was in the suitcases in the basement he was supposed to bring back? Rick Wilder was determined to find out.

He drove into Ravenswood in the dead of night and quickly found the address of the sagging house. He parked in the alley, quietly observing the other darkened houses. Nobody had lights on.

Wilder sneaked through the back yard, switched on a small pen flashlight, and found the back door key over the lintel right where Jenson had said it would be. He put the key into the lock and turned the latch. The door creaked open.

Once inside, he made sure that all the window shades were down and drapes closed.

He found the basement door at one end of the kitchen, and waving his flashlight one way and then the other, he made his way down the steps. To the right of the furnace was a false wall and door as Yip had described. Once inside, he carefully shut the door and flipped on the light switch. It was a dark room all right, with a series of rugs and drapes and women's underwear hanging on hangers against one wall. Under the sink, there were two suitcases, big, hard cover Samsonite suitcases. Those were what he'd been sent for. He pulled them out and switched off the light before opening the door and shoving them outside. Then he surveyed old bottles of chemicals on the counter beside the dark room sink, unstopped one of the bottles and turned it over on the counter. A thick amber liquid began to spread, and before Wilder left, he flicked a match into it.

It ignited with a whoosh, and Wilder left the basement with a suitcase in each hand, quietly made his way to the car, started it, and was long gone before the flames reached the upstairs levels and neighbors called the fire department.

# Chapter 33

Rick Wilder moseyed over to the bar where he knew Yip Jenson hung out. And sure enough, he sat in the back playing cards with his cronies. "Rick," Yip said, nodding at the man who'd come through the door.

"Jenson," Wilder said. Yip finished playing his hand, and then joined Wilder at a booth where the waitress had just placed a pitcher of beer and two glasses. Wilder poured out two glasses slowly. "Well, I got 'er done," he said.

"Heard all about it," Jenson said in return. "Well, not about you, of course, but about the deed itself. The sheriff says that the fire chief says it was arson."

"Do say," Wilder continued. "Guess you'll be wanting the suitcases. Got them stashed at my place. You know, it was a funny thing, that, eh, assignment," he said, smiling at Jenson. "You find things in old houses."

Yip narrowed his eyes at Wilder.

"Yep, funny things like these here pictures," and he took a few from his shirt pocket and slid them toward Jenson. Yip's eyes narrowed even further as he glanced at the pictures. Wilder put his hand over them and slid them back to his side of the table. "I suppose that old sheriff in Ravenswood would love to know about these, but I'm not going to tell him a thing."

"What's in a few dirty pictures?" Jenson growled.

"Nothing," Wilder said. "I mean, what's the harm of a few tootsies taking their clothes off? But, it's different, you know, when you find pictures of little girls standing beside a grown man, naked with his prick in her hand."

Yip turned the color of wallpaper paste.

"And then there's these lists of names and addresses of customers... See, I think that anyone in those pictures would probably want to pay a pretty penny to get them back. What do you think?" Wilder smiled a reptilian smile at Jenson.

Yip regained some of his color. So that was the game Wilder wanted to play. He looked at Wilder hard. "How much per picture?" he said.

"Oh, I'd say about one hundred dollars. Yeah, I'd say the kid's pictures would be worth about that." The men sat quietly sipping their beers. Then Jenson retrieved his wallet from his vest pocket, and handed Wilder a hundred dollar bill. Wilder carefully handed over one of the pictures from his pocket. "You want your regular order for Natalie?" Wilder asked.

"That will be good enough," Jenson said in a business voice. Then he got up and walked out of the bar.

Now, Yip Jenson had a definite problem. On the one hand, he reasoned, let Rick Wilder have the pictures. He should tell him to go to hell. He very likely was bluffing about going to Sheriff Conneally, because he'd have a lot of explaining to do, such as where did he exactly "get" the pictures and when?

On the other hand, this was nothing but trouble. Why hadn't the damn fool just burned the house down, as he was supposed to? Wouldn't you know that the weasel would pry those locked suitcases open. Yip figured that the pictures of naked women of the town might be risqué, but he didn't think it was a crime. But those damned little girls and the pictures of himself poised with them. That, he thought, could put him in jail for a few years.

The more he thought about it, the more he saw there was only one thing to do, and that was get rid of Wilder. He had to get the pictures from him, and the customer lists. And that meant all of them. And then, he had to get rid of Wilder once and for all. But how? Well, one thing was for sure. The world wouldn't miss one drug dealer, more or less. He couldn't just scare him or run him out of town by making a call to the police. That was dangerous. Wilder was a dangerous man, and he would come back to haunt him. Yip knew he could count on that. No, Wilder had to be killed. There was no other way, if Yip Jenson was going to live in peace and quiet for the rest of his life. But how to do it?

Yip Jenson knew a man who knew a man who knew a man' and it didn't take long for him to make contact with the third man in the chain of beasts. They met one moonless night on the wharf. "Say it can be done quietly?" Yip asked. "He lives in an apartment building."

"Quiet as can be," the other man said.

"And then you've got the right tools to do the rest of the job?"

"Yep, got 'em in a brief case."

"And you guarantee that I'll get my suitcases back, and I mean full. You're going to have to look around to make sure he hasn't taken half of them stuff out and stashed it someplace."

"I can do that," the other man said softly.

"$10,000? Half now, half when delievered."

"It's a deal," the man said, and the two of them shook hands.

Two weeks later, the Miami Herald ran a gruesome story about half of a body being found in a rundown apartment house. Whoever killed the man had done a very quiet, neat job of dismembering him. Nothing seemed disturbed in the apartment. The motive was mysterious. Body parts began showing up in a nearby swamp. The landlady identified what was left as being Rick Wilder, a nice tenant who paid his rent on time. "My God!" Yip Jenson quipped as he read the paper at the pool hall that afternoon while sipping cold beer. "What is this world coming to?"

# Chapter 34

Yip had gotten careless and had forgotten about a bunch of his latest pictures before he left town. He'd flung them in a canvas book bag to the back of his closet. Because of the direction of the wind that night, the west side of the house hadn't burned much. And when the fire marshal investigated, he found a few things in the bedroom closet including this bag which he promptly brought to Sheriff Conneally's office. "Seems there was a photography studio and dark room in the basement," the marshal said. "That's where the fire started, but we could make out burned out equipment, and cameras. Wonder what kind of pictures that old bastard was taking and developing down there? More like this, I would guess, but there's nothing left of them now."

Sheriff Conneally sat at his desk, and looked at the pictures of Selma Bagley, not out of lust but with the mind of a crime investigator trying to figure something out. Yip Jenson could have taken these pictures, probably did. Knowing what he did about Selma's behavior over the years, he wasn't surprised that she would pose nude for pictures.

But the question that kept playing about his mind was how many other pictures were in that house, pictures that had burned up in the fire? Yip Jenson had dated half the town, and that included married women who had no business seeing him in the afternoons while their husbands were at work. He'd received well meaning phone calls over the years from "concerned" neighbors. The problem was that there wasn't a law against adultery in the criminal code. You couldn't arrest someone for it. And besides, half of those "concerned" neighbors had been women who were concerned that it wasn't them! Or at least that was his opinion, and he chuckled thinking about it.

He couldn't talk to Selma Bagley about these pictures, since she had disappeared. He put the pictures back in a folder, placed the folder in his desk drawer, and locked the drawer. He'd just let all of this play on his mind and see if an answer would come.

# Chapter 35

Punky Rose Bagley sat at a table in the Ravenswood Library. Ever since October, she'd been reading romance novels from the adult section. She didn't want to check them out and take them home and have Aunt Haz see what she was reading. And she didn't want to share this new experience with Sheldon either. For the first time, she excluded him. And she felt guilty about it.

All she could think about these days was Jake Barnside, watching the colors of his eyes change as did his mood, just looking at his dark hair growing longer and curling around his ears. She loved the way he brushed it out of his face. And she loved looking at his arms, strong, muscled arms that looked as if they could crush the life out of you.

More and more, she thought about touching Jake. Just touching him, his hair, the slight cleft in his chin, running her thumb over his eyelids. She couldn't tell Sheldon about any of this. It made her feel breathless.

The romance novels were filled with passion and kisses and how beautiful and wonderful it all was. But was she abandoning Sheldon? He was the only boy in her life. She wondered if any girl would ever want to touch Sheldon with his scrawny arms and narrow shoulders?

Is that what her momma had wanted? To touch all those boyfriends who came to the house and stayed too long? But how could even her momma want to touch that creepy, old Yip Jenson? Had her momma really been in love with her father, Jackson Bagley, and could someone you really loved, when he just up and left you, would it make you stop caring about who touched you next?

One of the librarians walked by and smiled at Punky Rose. Punky Rose glanced up at the clock and saw that it was time to go. She carefully carried her math book, inside of which was the current romance novel, to the shelf and replaced the book in its niche. One thing for certain was that every book on the shelves had a different cover, but the stories were exactly alike, cookie cutter stories. She wondered if she should try her hand at writing one. Maybe she'd begin in her current journal and see where it went.

# Chapter 36

It was Saturday night in Ravenswood, Iowa, and Aunt Haz and Punky Rose sat watching TV. On the Evan Eugene Watkins Amateur Hour, beaming its way to Ravenswood from Minneapolis, Minnesota, a tall, lank woman sang a love song. She wasn't especially inspiring, but it got Punky Rose to thinking. She thought about Jake Barnside, and a new thought occurred to her. Aunt Haz. Why hadn't she ever married? She looked over at her aunt as if she was seeing her for the first time.

The lank woman on TV sang the final refrain of the song, "I'm in love, I'm in love, I'm in love." The audience clapped politely and a commercial came on. Aunt Haz got out of her chair and moved to the TV to turn it down. She hated commercials. "Aunt Haz," Punky Rose began, "were you ever in love?"

"In love?" Aunt Haz said, turning away from the TV to look at Punky Rose. She looked slightly away from

Punky Rose and sighed. "Well, I suppose I was at one time in my life."

"Why didn't you ever get married?" Punky Rose continued.

Haz settled back in her chair. The black and white images seemed ghostly on the screen, mouthing words that Haz and Punky Rose now could not hear.

"Well, I sure did have plenty of beaus," Haz said, thinking back. "I went to every dance there was in the county. And I had a date every Saturday night. Yes, I had plenty of fellas interested, but they all just seemed, "I don't know, nice to go out with, spend an evening with, but there was nobody I wanted to get serious about. After high school, I went to work in the office of John Deere, and I met plenty of people, too. I mean people not from here, people who I didn't grow up with. And my girl friends started getting married, and they teased me a lot about being an "old maid." I'd just tease them back. It was all good-hearted. And then, when I was thirty years old, I fell in love, really in love, for the first and last time."

She paused and looked down at her folded hands in her lap. Punky Rose didn't say a thing, waiting for her to continue. They sat quietly for a few moments before Haz began again. "Well, I guess you're old enough to hear this story," she said softly. "My true love's name was Caroline." And she stopped speaking. Punky Rose didn't get it at first. And then, as the idea seeped into her consciousness, the hair on the back of her neck began to prickle, and she looked at her aunt quizzically and intently. Aunt Haz didn't look at her, but continued to look at her folded hands. "Her name was Caroline," she said again firmly. "I didn't know you could have the kind of feelings that I felt for her, and she felt the same way about me. We saw each other quietly, of course. People thought we were just good friends. Well, we were. We were the best of friends. Oh my, the conversations that we had about just everything. You know, the smallest thing would happen at work, and I couldn't wait to tell Caroline all about it, like the time that Marv Shay bought the manure spreader and thought he got snookered on the price, and when the management wouldn't do anything about it, he pulled it into town full of shit and parked it right in front of the dealership! Oh my, we laughed about that for six months or more."

"Did you grow up together?" Punky Rose asked.

"Oh, no," Aunt Haz said. "See, Caroline's people weren't from Ravenswood. Her dad worked as a hired hand, and they came here for a job, I guess, when she was about finished with her senior year. They moved from pillar to post. After school let out, she got a job working for Hilda Meany cleaning house and taking care of her kids. Hilda always had a hired girl. But Caroline was an artist. She drew all the time, and you can't believe how good she was. She never took an art class in her life. It was natural talent. I met her right at the end of her senior year, but then I got busy and she got busy, and you know how things go.

But one night at the Grange Dance, she was there with some other girls, and I was there with some fella, and in those days, half of the time the girls danced with girls. Seems like the boys liked to stand off to the side or go outside for a snort. Well, Caroline and her friends were talking to me and my crowd, and a dance began, and Caroline grabbed me by the hand, and we started waltzing around the floor. And something turned over inside me, like my heart was all upside down, and I could hardly breathe. I could tell she felt the same way, and her arms closed tighter around me. When the music ended, we both were embarrassed, I think, I couldn't look at her for the rest of the night.

But she called me the next day, and we had coffee at the Rexall, and that started the whole thing. That just started everything. For the next year, we just couldn't get enough of each other. We were together every minute that we could manage. Caroline lived with her mom and dad. She helped them with her paycheck, and they needed it, but I had inherited this little house when my grandmother died, and so I lived alone. That made things easier, if you understand."

"You mean easier to be alone, and well, ah," Punky Rose didn't know how to say it, "like kiss and stuff?"

"Yes," Haz looked right at her. "Kiss and stuff. You see, love just happens at the oddest times. You go along in life, and then someone appears that makes your heart beat faster. Sometimes it happens early in life and sometimes, later, sometimes not at all. But when it happens, you know it. And it's the most wonderful feeling in the world.

"Well, what happened?" Punky Rose asked.

"As I said," Aunt Haz continued, "Caroline was an artist, and she just couldn't stand the idea that she was going to clean houses and take care of kids the rest of her life. She wasn't good at typing or business, like I was. Her big dream was to go to Kansas City, enroll in the art school there, and have a studio, and spend the rest of her life drawing her pictures, portraits, and still lifes, and everything. She wanted me to go with her, but I guess I was just too afraid of leaving my security, this house, my town, my job, I just couldn't leave Ravenswood. And Caroline couldn't stay. We parted. That's all I can say.

Her folks moved on, and Caroline moved on. And I did not. I've never met another person like her, another person that made me feel the way she did. So, I never married or had another love affair, except for one other person. There's only one other person I love as much as I loved Caroline. Can you guess who?"

"Nope," Punky Rose squinted her eyes at the question.

"Well, it's you, Punky Rose Bagley," Aunt Haz said. "You know, when someone in the family had to take care of you, I was about the only one who could really do it. But what did I know about raising a child? And you were a peculiar child at that. I didn't look forward to it. But I have to say that I've come to love you just as if you were my very own, Punky Rose. You're the dearest person in the world to me now."

"I'm glad you came and got me that day, too," Punky Rose said in a husky voice. She knew the tears were coming for both of them, and she reached for the Kleenex box on the side table. She pulled out a few and handed it over to Haz.

"Well, ain't we a pair," Aunt Haz said through her tears.

"We sure are," sputtered Punky Rose. Just then the doorbell rang, and Sheldon came through the door.

"What's a matter?" he asked, concerned at seeing the two of them wiping their eyes.

"Oh, nothing, the story on TV was a sad one," Aunt Haz said. But when Sheldon turned to look at the silent TV, all he saw was the Texas Two-Shooters, a cowboy band, smiling out at the audience, and strumming their guitars with great zest.

# Chapter 37

Punky Rose Bagley opened her journal and began to write about love. She labeled one page Momma, another Sheldon, a third, Aunt Haz, and finally on a fourth page, she wrote Jake Barnside in back, hand, something she'd been experimenting with. She felt very confused about the whole concept. She wanted to sort it all out.

Her mother. Well, she was supposed to love her mother, but how did she really feel? She remembered crying a lot as a little kid because her mother ignored her. She remembered the string of boyfriends who took up her mother's time. What were mothers supposed to do for their children? Well, for one thing they were supposed to pay attention to them, but beyond that, they were supposed to put a roof over their heads. OK, Selma had done that. They were supposed to feed them, make sure they had clothes, and went to school.

She remembered the refrigerator and cupboards in which there was nothing to eat. She remembered taking her little lunch box with Tinker Bell on the lid to school because that's what all the kids did. But when lunch time came, much of the time, there was nothing in hers. That's when Sheldon had begun sharing his lunch with her, sandwiches, chips, apples, a thermos of milk. Mrs. McNamara had caught on and began sending double lunches. Sheldon would open his lunch box and quietly slip half of its contents into hers. Neither of them wanted the other kids or teachers to catch on.

Clothes? Those rejects from the Salvation Army shop? Well, if that's all she had, Punky Rose had decided very early on to act as if it was exactly what she chose herself. She would make her tacky clothes an emblem of pride.

Had her mother fixed up a little room for her like Aunt Haz had done? Nope. In the second bedroom, she had slept on a mattress. She was lucky to have a tattered quilt to wrap up in during the winter, another Salvation Army find. And somewhere along the line, she had stopped crying and had realized that she had to take care of herself. Her momma wasn't going to take care of her. It was as if at this point, she had just walked into a giant freezer and become frozen with any emotion toward her mother. She closed off her mind to Selma's life even if she had to live in the same house with her. Punky's life was centered around Sheldon, her life at school, and the books that she read at school and the library. More and more, her mother didn't exist.

So, did she love her mother? She felt nothing when she thought about her. It didn't matter if Selma was out in that old farm house, in the hospital, or gone. It just didn't matter.

Next, she thought about Sheldon. Up until this year, he had been the object of what you might call love. He was a friend that you could trust with anything like the fact that you didn't have food in your Tinker Bell lunch box. He never made fun of you, or told you that you were stupid. He never mentioned your clothes. He didn't ask about your mother. He never lied. He was a friend that you could tell any secret you had to, that was if you had any secrets. She'd do anything to help Sheldon out, and she'd sock anybody who said a bad thing about him. She guessed that was love. She loved Sheldon McNamara. He was the brother that she never had.

The third page was devoted to Aunt Haz. She had cried when Haz told her story and said she loved her. She had let Aunt Haz see her cry three times: one after the Indian Trail discovery, once when she got the red coat, and last night when Aunt Haz had said she loved her. Why did that make her cry? It was something about the way Aunt Haz said it, like a hand reached right into your chest and squeezed your heart. What did that mean?

Well, Aunt Haz had signed on to being her guardian. She fixed up this little room for her. She bought her new underwear, socks, pajamas, that plaid skirt and sweater. She bought her new clothes, good, sturdy things, pretty things, and she just put them in the dresser drawers most of the time without saying a word. She cooked good meals and saw to it that Punky Rose had money for a cafeteria lunch at school every day. She had treats, like the ice cream that they shared before going to bed. And best of all, really, was the fact that she talked to Punky Rose.

Aunt Haz was a talker, all right. She talked about things that happened at work and at the church and about the neighbors. She told stories about old times. She knew just about everybody in town. She was the one to tell Punky all about Jake Barnside. She asked Punky Rose what she wanted for supper, how she did on her English test, if she was writing in her journal, what was new at the library. Aunt Haz talked and talked and talked. And about half of the time, Punky Rose just shut her ears to the noise. But more and more, she found herself listening, joining in, having an opinion, and then beginning to feel again. It made her feel comfy when she heard Aunt Haz begin to talk, whether she was exclaiming over the eggs she got at the farmer's market or was telling a good juicy story about some poor soul she had known. That comfy feeling must be a kind of love.

And then there was Jake. The feelings she felt inside were like the ones she read about in the romance novels. Sometimes, he was just good, old Jake, friend and protector of children. That's what Sheldon said. But other times, she felt fluttery around him, nervous. And then there'd be the times she wanted to touch him, maybe even kiss him. When these thoughts came, she felt embarrassed and confused and tried to get those feelings to behave, stop, go away, but they never really did. Sheldon had picked up on this right away, of course. You couldn't put anything over on him. But he was too much of a good friend to have ever brought it up again after their fight at Thanksgiving. And now she'd found out that these romantic type feelings could be between two women. Nobody was writing romance novels about that!

She jotted down her observations beneath each name and then closed her journal and put it in her drawer. Valentine's Day was only a few weeks off. Maybe she'd make Sheldon, Aunt Haz, and Jake a valentine just as she had done in first grade, with red construction paper, and lace paper doilies, and glitter. She smiled at the idea before turning off her light.

# Chapter 38

I t was a warm, April day, a Saturday, when Punky Rose Bagley came out of the bathroom with a frown on her face. "Making waffles," Aunt Haz called from the kitchen. When she turned to smile at Punky, she noticed something was wrong. "What's the matter?" she asked. "What's with the long face?"

"Punky sat down at the table slowly like an old woman. "Well, I think it started," she said.

"What started?" Aunt Haz quizzed, and then she stopped and put her hand to her mouth. "Oh," she said. "Oh. It."

"Can I have some coffee this morning?" Punky Rose asked as if the weight of the world was bogging her down. Aunt Haz had been allowing Punky to have coffee since Christmas if she put lots of milk in it.

"Sure, honey, let me pour you a mug," Aunt Haz said. "How do you feel?"

"Kinda crampy," Punky Rose said taking the mug from Aunt Haz.

"Well, that's the way it is," Aunt Haz said. "Drink that warm white coffee. It will make you feel better. Did you use the pad and belt that I put in the closet?"

"Yeah," Punky Rose said, hand clasping the mug.

"Them waffles can wait for a few minutes," Aunt Haz said, pouring herself some coffee, and sitting down opposite Punky Rose. "You know what this means," she asked. Punky shook her head. "It means that today you become a woman, a bonafide woman. Childhood is over. It's a wonderful thing, Punky Rose. Oh, I know that people make jokes about it and some people call it the curse, but it means that someday you can have babies. It is a blessed thing. Some girls have a little pain with it, like you're having. They feel crampy, like you say, but all you have to do is take an aspirin and you'll be just fine. I think that this calls for a celebration."

"A celebration!" Punky Rose said squinting up her eyes.

"Yes, a celebration," Aunt Haz said. "Now, I think that I'll make a coconut cake, a layer cake just for the occasion. I think that Gwen McNamara said she had some early lilacs blooming. We could fix a vase of them, and we could put some decorations up, and…" she trailed off looking at Punky's face. It looked as if she might start to cry.

"Why, what's the matter, honey?" she said in a comforting voice. "This is the most natural thing on earth."

"I suppose that I shouldn't tell Sheldon about it," she sniffed.

"Well, I don't know why not," Aunt Haz said. "Maybe, we'll invite him to have cake with us."

"I don't want Jake to know," Punky said suddenly in a panicked voice. "I don't want him to know anything about it."

"Well, sure. That's OK," Aunt Haz said. "This is personal, I know. But instead of looking at this like you have a disease or something the way my mother acted when I told her, I want this to be a good experience for you."

The next afternoon, promptly at 2:00, Gwen McNamara showed up at Aunt Haz's house, along with Theresa Barnside. Gwen had a vase of lilacs and Theresa had made a crown of lace and braided ribbons for Punky Rose to wear. Sheldon had decided that this was a woman thing. He told Punky they'd talk about it later, but he'd feel funny being the only guy with three old women and the young princess maiden! The women came into the kitchen hugging and exclaiming over Punky Rose who didn't know what to say or how to act. Theresa put the crown on Punky's head, and all the women held hands in a circle around the table as Aunt Haz welcomed Punky

Rose Bagley into the society of women. "A blessed young woman joins us today," she said and each woman said, "Amen." Gwen made the sign of the cross over Punky's forehead, and Theresa read a little poem about womanhood that she had torn out of the Reader's Digest. Aunt Haz said she had a surprise and brought out a tray with tall fluted glasses on it and took a cold bottle of champagne out of the fridge. "I never could open one of these here things," she quipped.

"Give it ta me," Gwen said, "and hand me that dish towel." Gwen unwrapped the wire over the cork, and with the dish towel wrapped around the cork, she worked it back and forth gently until it popped from the bottle. "There," she laughed and began slowly pouring the bubbly into the glasses. Each woman and Punky was handed a glass, and then Aunt Haz said they had to make toasts.

"I hope only sunshine and good fortune for you all the days of your life," said Aunt Haz. Everybody sipped.

"I hope long life and good friends," Gwen said, and they sipped.

"May you find happiness in all that you do," Theresa quipped, and they sipped. Then, they all began to tell stories about their experiences with IT, many of them very funny, and the more they sipped (Gwen refilling their glasses), the funnier the stories got.

"Time to cut the cake," Aunt Haz announced bringing the lovely two layer white cake to the table. She'd dribbled dark, bitter chocolate over the top. Everyone admired the cake, and then Punky Rose was asked to make the first cut.

The ladies finished off the afternoon with coffee, more hugs for Punky, and then each made her way home. Aunt Haz began to put things away and clean up the kitchen. "Think I'll take a hot bath," Punky told her taking her crown off and hanging it on the hook on the wall where the embroidered dish towels hung. "And thanks, Aunt Haz," she said feeling all sparkly inside. Then she gave her a quick hug before moving towards the bathroom. Haz had tears in her eyes as she turned back to the kitchen sink.

# Chapter 39

It was mid-May when Aunt Haz decided to tidy up the basement and go through Selma's things. "It's time," she said, mostly to herself.

"Time for what?" Punky asked her.

"Well, you know I've been wanting to clean out the basement, get things organized. It won't be long before we have to take the outdoor furniture to the backyard and get the screen windows out. And there's those boxes of your mother's. Let's face it. She's not coming back. We need to go through those boxes and get rid of things. Do you think you're up to helping?"

"I guess so," Punky Rose said, frowning at her aunt.

"Well, let's start," Aunt Haz said. "Now finish your sandwich, and then we'll go down to the basement. It'll be nice down there this afternoon, nice and cool."

And so that's how Punky Rose found herself unpacking the big boxes that had set behind the furnace for nine months. A big oak table sat in the middle of the room, and it was onto this that Haz and Punky Rose sorted the contents of the boxes. Dresses and lingerie went in one pile, the few blankets and linens in another. When they came to a box of jewelry, Haz and Punky Rose sat down on the old dining room chairs to go through the box. "Hmm," said Haz. "Just costume jewelry in here. I wonder what she did with her mother's things. I know she had a good string of pearls and a Boliva watch. Also some small diamond earrings." And she pawed through the mess of trinkets and plastic necklaces, trying to sort things out. Finally, underneath the tangle, they found the pearls, watch, and earrings.

"Now, you need to keep these things," Haz told Punky, laying them to one side. "These were your grandmother's, and she was a lovely lady. Anything of your mother's that you want to keep as a treasure?"

Punky Rose chose a fake pink coral necklace, each bead looking like a small rose, and a blue brooch that glittered in the light. It was as big as a child's fist and had an intricate design. "This is about all," she said.

"Well, let's get to those boxes of shoes," Haz said. Then we can repack everything and take the boxes to the Salvation Army. Too bad there's nothing for your hope chest."

"But I don't have a hope chest," Punky Rose said.

"Well, we'll have to get you one." Aunt Haz smiled at her. "Can't have hope without a hope chest!"

Aunt Haz dug into the bottom of one of the boxes, and came up with ten shoeboxes. She set them on the table and took off their lids one by one. Black patent leather, soft blue sandals, white spikes. "Size seven," Aunt Haz said. "What size do you wear?"

"Size seven," Punky Rose said. "But I sure don't want any of these things."

"Oh, that's right," Haz laughed. "You prefer worn out tennies."

"What's wrong with that?" Punky Rose shot back.

"Nothing." Haz laughed again. "Actually, it's your signature fashion statement." And now Punky Rose had to laugh with her.

"Now, what's this?" Haz said, holding up a shoebox all taped up with duct tape. She turned the box this way and that. An address to Selma Bagley was written with a big black marker on top. The name of the post office where it was mailed from was smudged. She couldn't read it. "Get me them shears," Haz told Punky. Punky went over to where Haz's old Singer sewing machine sat against a wall, and opened the side drawer. She pulled out a pair of scissors and handed them to Haz. Haz worked diligently for almost five minutes, cutting all the layers of tape, but finally she got the lid off the box. And then she almost had a heart attack, for what she saw was neat stacks of one thousand dollar bills. "My God, what's this?" she hissed.

Punky Rose stuck her nose close and whistled. "Rat's ass!"

"What on earth," Aunt Haz said again, pulling out the bundles. Silently she began to count, laying each bundle carefully on the table. "Punky Rose, do you know how much money this is?" she asked with frightened eyes. "There's one hundred thousand dollars here." Punky Rose couldn't believe her eyes. She sat stone still.

"Now where on earth would Selma get a bundle like this?" Haz picked up the box and lid again and began examining it closely. "Who would send her a box of money? Why didn't she open it? It wonder if it's real or counterfeit?"

"What's that?" Punky Rose said, pointing to a small scrap of paper peeking out from under the last stack of money that Haz had pulled from the box. Haz quickly pulled it out from under the rubber band. She smoothed it, read it, and handed it to Punky Rose. Punky Rose read it several times and then looked at her aunt.

"Oh, Punky Rose," Haz said slowly, sitting back in her chair and taking off her glasses. You know what this means?"

"Not Sheriff Conneally," Punky Rose said.

"I'm afraid so," Haz said, "and he's not going to like it. Don't say a word even to Sheldon, and let me try to figure out what to do."

It was Sunday afternoon, and rain was predicted. The weather had gone from hot and windy to cool and rainy in the last hour. The old saying in Iowa was that if you didn't like the weather all you had to do was wait a day or so and it would change. Sheriff Conneally had just finished a dinner of fried chicken and potato salad. He wished that he could remain sitting at home with his pants unbuttoned, sipping a beer, and watching a baseball game on TV. But instead, he was calling on Haz Limestone, who seemed to have some new problem. Another problem, and sitting in the middle of it was that Bagley girl again. He rang Haz's doorbell, and she answered the door. "Hello there," she said, "good of ya to come. I've got something in the basement that I think you should see." And she led the way through the house to the basement door in the kitchen. Punky Rose followed them downstairs.

"We was cleaning out some boxes," Haz began. "These were Selma's things," she continued, "and I thought it was high time to get them passed along. No sense letting them sit here for another year. But then we came to this here box," and she shoved the duct-taped box over to Sheriff Conneally. "I cut the tape myself," Haz said. "It didn't seem that it was ever opened."

Sheriff Conneally took off the lid and let out a snort. "My God," he said, taking the bundles of money out of the box and stacking them on the table.

"There's one hundred thousand dollars in them bundles," Haz said. Punky Rose just looked worried. The sheriff pulled his glasses from his shirt pocket and put them on. Then he scrutinized the lid and address. "I couldn't make out where it was sent from," Haz said. "But we found this note at the bottom of the box." The sheriff took it from Haz and read:

"Dear Selma,

I finally got a nest egg. Keep this under wraps. I'll be in touch any day now.

JB"

"Jackson Bagley?" he asked, squinting at Haz.

"Looks like it," she said.

"But he never contacted Selma, did he?" he asked. "Did he ever contact you or Punky Rose, since Selma was, well, was away?"

"Never done," Haz said. Punky Rose shook her head no.

"And Selma never mentioned anything about a box of money?" he continued.

"No, she didn't. Of course, she wasn't communicating at all," Haz said. "And if she had talked about a box of money to her doctors, wouldn't you think they'd ask me about it?"

"Well, you never know about that," the sheriff said. "With confidentiality and all. Suppose I better have a talk with her doctor. What's his name?"

"Swanson," Punky Rose said matter-of-factly,

"Yes," Haz said, looking knowingly at Punky Rose. "It was Swanson."

"Do you think it's real?" Haz ventured.

"Looks real," the sheriff said, "but I'd better have that checked too. You say it's been sitting here for a year?"

"Yep," Haz said, "ever since we packed her stuff after she went away."

"Have you told anybody else about this?" he asked.

"No, we haven't," Haz said, looking directly at Punky Rose, who nodded a "no" vote.

"I think that I had better put it in the jail's safe," the sheriff said. "Get me a brown shopping bag or something like it. I'll just mosey up to the office and lock this up. And I'll be in touch within a few days. Now, mum's the word." And with that he placed the box and money and lid inside a paper bag that Punky Rose retrieved for him. "Good afternoon, ladies," he said smiling. With that he left their house.

# Chapter 40

Sheriff Conneally checked his police reports, his bulletins of people wanted, and he could find nothing in the last ten years that would indicate that the money Haz Limestone had was part of a bank robbery, or a robbery of any kind. Next, he'd checked several of the bills pulled out of stacks at random for a test at the bank. Then he dialed Cherokee State Hospital and asked to speak to Dr. Swanson. He was lucky. The doctor was in, had just finished making rounds, and came quickly to the phone. Sheriff Conneally explained the situation. One hundred thousand dollars in cash had been found in Selma Bagley's stored clothing. Her aunt had been cleaning things out when she found the money. Had Selma ever mentioned money, a fortune, a shoe box sent to her through the mail, anything like this?

Dr. Swanson gave the sheriff his regular speech about confidentiality, but put the sheriff on hold while he asked his office assistant to find the Bagley file. He told the sheriff that it might take a few minutes, as the assistant would have to go to the basement where the files were kept for those patients who no longer were at the hospital. Sheriff Conneally said he'd be glad to wait, and he did. He read through police files and bulletins again, while he held the receiver to his ear. Nothing. There was nothing that he could connect with this shoebox of money.

Finally, the doctor came back on the phone. The sheriff could hear him rustling through papers. "Hmm," he said several times. "You know, I'll have to read this closely to make sure, but the scanning of my notes sure doesn't indicate that we ever talked about money. Do you want me to do a more thorough search?" he asked.

"I'd appreciate it," the sheriff said. "I have a shoebox full of one thousand dollar bills sent to Selma Bagley, apparently never opened, and apparently sent by her husband who abandoned her years before. And as far as we know, he never showed up to claim the money or make a new life with Selma. Of course, if Selma never opened the box and never read the note, she wouldn't have been expecting him, either. It seems odd that a woman would get a mysterious box all duct-taped together in the mail, and not be curious enough about it to open it."

"Not if you knew Selma," Dr. Swanson said. "If I come across anything interesting, I'll give you a call. Now, give me your phone number," and with that the call ended.

Why, when it came to this family, was there never an answer to the questions that came up? the sheriff thought. The car in the quarry, the man lurking around the Methodist church, the man on the Indian Trail, the pictures found in the burned-out house... Wait a minute! he thought. The man on the Indian Trail. Jackson Bagley says he found a grubstake. He sends his wife the box of money and says he'll be coming back to her soon. Selma doesn't open the box and, therefore, doesn't expect anything. She's dating Yip Jenson, who according to Haz dumps her, and she has a psychotic episode, as Dr. Swanson has indicated. Within a few months of her being signed in at Cherokee, the strange events begin happening, including an unidentified man being found dead. Then, there's the men's conversation in the park which includes talk about finding money. Next thing you know, Selma disappears with a new orderly at the hospital. Could there be a connection between the events? Sheriff Conneally thought it was time to have a talk with Haz and Punky Rose Bagley, one more time.

# Chapter 41

"I promised Aunt Haz that I would not say a word," Punky Rose told Sheridan a few days after the sheriff's visit. "But I just can't keep it to myself one more minute."

"You know that I keep secrets," Sheldon said importantly. The two of them were sitting at the Rexall having a chocolate malt and cheeseburgers on a Tuesday night.

"Well, we found something," Punky Rose began in a hushed voice, leaning towards Sheldon. "We found something in the basement in one of the boxes of my momma's clothes. It was a shoebox all wrapped up with duct tape with her address on one side. Never been opened, it seems, and when Aunt Haz cut it open, we found money."

"Money?" questioned Sheldon. "Whataha mean money?"

"Lots of one thousand bills, all rubber-banded together into neat stacks. Aunt Haz counted it. She says there's at least one hundred thousand dollars in that box." And she sat back a little, waiting for her story to sink in.

Sheldon just squinted back at her. "You sure you ain't telling me a whopper, something out of one of your stories?" he asked suspiciously.

"Nope, she said, looking superior.

"One hundred thousand dollars?" Sheldon turned his head and looked at her with glasses askew.

"One hundred thousand dollars," she said again.

Sheldon looked into his malt for a moment, before straightening his glasses and looking across the table again. It was like he could not comprehend what she was telling him. "There's more," she said.

"Oh, my God," he said softly.

"There was a note from Jackson Bagley in one of them stacks."

"Whad it say?" Sheldon asked quickly.

"It said that he had a grubstake, momma was to keep the box, and he'd contact her soon. That's what it said," she added.

"But he never showed up?" Sheldon said. "Until... " and his voice trailed off.

"That's what I'm thinking," said Punky Rose. "He showed up all right, but it was too late. She was gone and her things cleared out of the house. And somebody else must have known about the money, and that Jackson

Bagley was nosing around and that's why he got killed the way he did."

"Oh, Saint Suds," Sheldon exclaimed. His eyes were big and round behind his glasses. "Jeeze, this is getting creepy!" he said, shaking his head.

"Creepy," Punky Rose echoed. "Aunt Haz will have a fit if she thinks I've told. The sheriff is investigating and everything."

"Oh, not the sheriff again," Sheldon said, slurping into his malt.

"Yes, the sheriff again," said Punky Rose, chewing on the last of her hamburger.

# Chapter 42

Sheriff Conneally headed to the south of town to have another talk with Hazel Limestone. She welcomed him and poured him some coffee as they sat around the yellow Formica table. Punky Rose was off somewhere with Sheldon. "It seems that the money is real," he began. "But I can't trace where it came from. Now assuming that the man on the trail was Jackson Bagley, and he's dead, and Selma is God knows where, and of course she doesn't know anything about the money anyway, it seems that this money should be put in a trust fund for Punky Rose. I've checked with the DA, and he agrees that it's a strange case, but it's reasonable to put the money in a trust that Punky can draw from when she's eighteen. You, being her guardian, would have to sign off on the trust, and you can actually say that any withdrawals have to be approved by you until she's twenty-five, or something like that. The county lawyer can set up the trust."

Hazel thought about it for a moment and then nodded her head. It was a reasonable plan and she thanked the sheriff for all of his help.

"I hope that I never hear of the name Punky Rose Bagley, or Sheldon McNamara, or Jake Barnside, unless they did something spectacular in school! he chuckled.

"Well, I hope that the only time I see you is in church," Aunt Haz chuckled back. The sheriff sipped his coffee.

"It sure has been an eventful year for your family and for this town," he said.

"Hasn't it though," Aunt Haz mused, refilling their cups.

# Chapter 43

A few days later, the teenagers had a surprise. Jake Barnside called Punky Rose and asked to meet her and Sheldon. Punky Rose and Sheldon walked to the park wondering what Jake had in store. They got there a little before four, the appointed time, and sat in the swings. Jake was nowhere to be found.

And then a 1957 bright red Chevy cruised up to the parking spaces adjacent to the park, and Jake casually got out of the driver's seat. He almost swaggered over to the swings, twirling a key ring in his hands. Punky Rose and Sheldon just sat there staring.

"Like my new car?" Jake asked.

"Wow," Sheldon breathed out. "Is that really yours? Where did you get it?"

"Bought it over at a used car lot in Fort Nelson. Ain't it a beauty?"

"It sure is," Sheldon said. "Can we go for a ride in it?"

Punky Rose didn't know what to say, so she just got up and walked over to the car and climbed into the back seat. Sheldon got into the passenger side, and Jake got into the driver's side and started the car up. The motor hummed like a contented cat.

The three of them drove all over Ravenswood, up and down the streets, before Jake pulled onto the highway and revved it up to sixty miles per hour. "Sure is smooth for an old car," Sheldon said. Jake began telling him all about the restoration that is previous owner had done. He described the engine and transmission in technical terms which Sheldon appeared to understand. Punky Rose couldn't make any sense of the conversation.

"You're pretty quiet back there," Jake said, looking at her in the rear view mirror. Punky Rose just smiled back at him.

"How you gonna pay for it?" she asked, finally finding her voice.

"I got full time hours at the Creamery this summer," he said, "plus I'd saved up a little."

"Guess we have a new form of transportation for now," Sheldon laughed. "This is a little classier than bikes!"

"Nothing wrong with bikes," Jake said stopping back at the park. "Well, I gotta get ready for work. See you too," and the kids exited the car and waved him off.

Punky Rose sat down in one of the swings and Sheldon sat in the other. There was only a few more days of school and then they'd be out for the summer. "Whada you gonna do this summer?" she asked Sheldon.

"Keep off the Indian Trail," he quipped and the two of them had to laugh.

"No, really, whada you gona do?" she persisted.

"Well, Conor says that I can have his lawn customers. He's mowed lawns for five or six people for three years now, but this summer he's going to work at the Dairy Queen. He says I can take over for him if I want."

"Mowing lawns all summer. Sounds like a lotta work," Punky Rose said.

"Yeah, but the money's good. I can get $5.00 per lawn and an extra $2.50 if I trim and stuff. That could be $30.00 a week, not bad money, really."

"I think that I'll volunteer at the library," Punky Rose said thoughtfully. Mrs. Mason, the librarian, asked me if I wanted to help. She said that I spent all my time at the library anyway… I might as well work there. Well, I mean, it wouldn't be for money, it would be volunteering."

"What would you do?" Sheldon asked.

"Oh, shelve books, and straighten the magazine section, and she might even show me how to check out books. I could learn a lot about how to run a library. And besides I get to be around all those books!"

"Hope this summer turns out to be better than the last one," Sheldon said thoughtfully.

"Couldn't be worse," Punky Rose answered him. The kids left the park thinking about the time that stretched ahead.

That night in her journal, Punky Rose wrote:

"Just think. One year ago, I was answering the door in that saggy, old farmhouse, telling the social worker that my momma was sick. And now, I am living in a nice house with my great aunt that I didn't even know a year ago. And she's kind and nice and sees to it that I have clean clothes. She cooks real good too.

I don't know where my momma is. Aunt Haz says that sometimes children come through people, but they aren't a part of those people. Their souls aren't mixed up together, or something like that. My soul sure isn't mixed up with Jackson Bagley, the poor man, or my mother. Never was. Maybe, my soul was supposed to come through Aunt Haz, but she loved Caroline, so I had to wait for awhile until I could be part of her. That's what I figger happened. Think part of my soul is a sister to Sheldon. That's for sure. Nobody could have a greater pal than Sheldon. And then this year I met up with Jake Barnside. But I don't know what to say about that."

Punky Rose put her journal into her desk drawer, turned off the light and lay down on her bed. She could see the stars high up in the night sky, and she liked looking at them. They were always there, something that you could count on unlike a lot of people that you had to put up with. And she guessed that that was about the most important thing in the whole wide world, knowing people that you could count on. Yep, that was the most important thing.

# About the Author

Barbara O'Donnell is a published writer, story teller in the old Celtic tradition, teacher, and owner of Pusheen Press. Although born in Sacramento during WWII, she spent her formative years in rural, small town Iowa, and this is the setting of much of her work. Currently, she teaches at Sacramento State University and lives in midtown Sacramento in a 1916 bungalow with her family of cats!